C000061610

About the author

Patrice Chaplin is an interna...ionally renowned playwright and author who has published more than 36 books, plays and short stories. Her most notable work includes *Albany Park, Siesta* – which was made into a film staring Jodi Foster and Isabella Rossellini with music by Miles Davis – *Into the Darkness Laughing, Hidden Star, Night Fishing, Death Trap* and *City of Secrets.*

As a Bohemian in Paris during the 50's and 60's, she spent time with Jean Paul Sartre and Simone de Beauvoir. She was married to Charlie Chaplin's son, Michael, and during her avant-garde journeys through occult circles her friends included Salvador Dali, Jean Cocteau – who gave her a starring role in one of his films – Lauren Bacall, Miles Davis and experts on the esoteric practices of the Kabbalah in Spain.

As an accomplished writer, Patrice has contributed to many collections of short stories, including *Black Valentine* and *The Minerva Book of Short Stories 1.* Her plays, documentaries, and short stories have been extensively written and adapted for radio. The short story *Night in Paris* has been translated in many countries, and other short stories of hers have appeared in magazines and newspapers, including *The Independent.*

Patrice's stage play *From the Balcony* was commissioned by The National Theatre in London in conjunction with BBC Radio 3, and was performed at the Cottesloe Theatre.

Patrice is the director of The Bridge, a non-profit organization that leads workshops based in the performing arts as a new and unique way to help fight addiction.

To Yogi –

THE
FORTUNE
SELLER

PATRICE CHAPLIN

All Best Wishes

Patrice C –

SESHAT PRESS

22 – 6 – 15

CONTENTS

CHAPTER I

I LET THE PHONE ring three times and answered as they'd
told me. 'Welcome to the Fate Line. My name is Isis.' I added
something else because I didn't feel I'd come across well enough
and my name was crazy. I said, 'Have you been on line before?'

She laughed. 'Hasn't everybody?' She was elegant and the
voice belonged in nice places. My hand actually shook as I cut
a pack of tarot cards into three. My other held the receiver to
my ear. I was grateful the woman couldn't see me. The set of
cards in front of me meant nothing and I was impatient for some
sign, some word. Into my mind arrived the image of sheep, grey
fluffy creatures and I drew them on the paper as though to get
rid of them. I should be getting love, work, money. I got sheep.
How much was my subconscious mind going to screw me up? I
needed this job. What were the words they'd told me to follow?
Attune to the person's voice and see what comes into your mind?
I looked again at the cards and my betraying mouth said, 'sheep.'
I was a loser of course. How else had I ended on this line?

'Sheep?' She was prepared to be patient.

I drew another animal and a square that could be a hut. I
was worried my voice would shake. 'Several sheep and a hut.' I
didn't think I'd ever heard the name of such a building. I hoped,

how I did that the management were not listening in.

'A sheep croft,' she informed me, then laughed.

Her laugh was natural, her voice classless. She'd been on the call precisely two minutes. Quickly I told her happy stuff which I'd heard from other psychics. I read off the cards and stuck with red aces and red coins. She was getting good news, she must stay on line. The red coins looked better than the others. In fact they looked like high money and I didn't have to pretend to be psychic to see that.

'Am I paying this out or getting it in?'

'In.' What else should I say?

'On Isis you are priceless.'

'The coins are showing on every card.'

'Oh don't bother with that Isis. You're too good for that.'

I couldn't make sense of that compliment. She didn't sound sarcastic.

'Can you see where these sheep are?' Her voice was teasing.

'Scotland,' I said, promptly. Did they have sheep in Scotland? A psychic mind should be open to receiving images and messages from the spirit world. Mine was blank. 'A place in your childhood,' I added, needing to keep the reading going. We've all had childhoods and much of it not recallable. 'It could be a picture in a children's book.' I gave her every option.

'Thank you.' She was going to hang up.

Please don't put that phone down. Six minutes? I need twenty! 'The man, the man,' I said, suddenly.

Why was she on line? It had to be a man. Money. Career. Something lost. This was worse than the dream where I went on stage and had no idea of the lines or even the play. 'He wears something that makes him look like . . .' What?

'Could it be a sheep?' At least one of us was having a good time. Her laugh filled another thirty seconds. 'Perhaps he wears a wig, Isis? A legal person.' She was helping now.

'How about a judge?'

Real laughter now. 'Thank you, Isis.' And she was gone. I

hated the silence.

I'd managed to keep her for eight minutes and earned nearly £3. I'd forgotten to ask her date of birth. I'd also forgotten to give her the clairvoyant's choice. Romance, wealth, luck, to stop her from hanging up. This was 8.15 p.m. on 1 February 1998. She came back some weeks later and I didn't remember her.

'You got sheep.' Then I remembered her laugh.

I was told you never forget your first reading as you never forget your first love, but I had no idea what I'd said to her or even her name. I vaguely remembered my drawing of sheep as though putting an image on paper gave some sort of credibility. I'd probably binned it among dozens of other scraps of paper with names and dates of birth.

I was reading the cards better these days and even managed to make a clattering noise of a pack being cut and the sound of a genuine shuffle. I could still see her money-happy spread.

'Oh, come on.' She did have a lovely laugh. 'You're too good for that.'

Had she said that before?

'I want you to read for my husband. He's a total disbeliever in these matters. I'll give you a little help. One or two things you might say.'

And I thought I really had made it as a clairvoyant. Someone wanting a reading with me. I'd cut my teeth, as the gypsies say. She told me to write down the messages she was about to give me and say they came from spirit. I was to remember her name was Lou. To keep it going longer I asked why.

'Why?' She sounded surprised.

She thought I was questioning the idea. I'd meant why did I have to write them down.

'Because he needs cheering up. And we want him to believe in the other world, don't we?'

The messages meant nothing to me and I started to say so. 'You have such a lovely voice,' she cut in. 'He'll believe you. Remember my name. Good luck, Isis.'

And so began a course of events beyond belief, deadly, that not even a psychic could have foreseen.

*

I'd hit hard times. It happened as it often does, quickly, and the money and success had simply gone out like a tide and would surely come in again. For now I was stranded high and dry with all the usual habits and expectations, the way of life of someone who had definitely made it. The money went first, the habits last and it still took some months to realise the tide was not going to come in again, bringing with it my bountiful life. I was thirty for the public but Ray started saying I looked my real age. He said for now I should forget performing and get a job, any job. I thought I should get another boyfriend.

'You rose up quick but the coming down was quicker.'

I'd expected something more supportive from him but he was now paying the bills.

'You should have saved.'

Of course I didn't save. I didn't see it coming. I'm not psychic.

An unfortunate boast as it turned out and hardly a day later I waited my turn to audition for a London show. Chorus? I couldn't go much lower. A girl I knew from the old days showed me an ad for a psychic line and said if I knew in advance what was coming up it wouldn't be such a shock. I don't go in for catastrophe thinking, I told her.

'You might now.' She looked a little grim.

I didn't bother with the audition and phoned the line. I got Betty, known professionally as Angel, predominantly fake, but just able to cover it. I liked her warmth but wasn't impressed with the reading. I tried two more and wanted to know only one thing. Will I get a starring role now? The first one said I knew how to please a man. 'You give him what he wants.' Had I dialled a sex line? I'd expected a psychic to speak with ancient intonation, in touch with another world. This one spoke as though he was selling paint. The laugh was terrible. The second, too bright and cheerful, said I'd live in Tunbridge Wells. 'A classy house with a red front door and a gold knocker.'

I wouldn't be dead in Tunbridge Wells. English small towns had never been my thing. The psychics were so bad I could surely not do worse myself. How much did they get? Could I work as a psychic reader?

It was no more than a frivolous thought coming from the shock of how bad things actually were. Ray had suggested I get a job, any job. Maybe that was better than going further downhill in a career I loved. Doing something different would not stir up the pain of failure as for example backing singer or club presenter and that came next. I'd do the line if I could get on it for at most a week. Was I psychic? Was the person who said I'd live behind a red door in Tunbridge Wells? Who could prove him wrong? Only the future.

What exactly was the line? Having had some dealing with Betty I got her private number. She said the company run by Sadie Chill began some years ago in a modest room in Bloomsbury with four readers and four phones was now big business. Two hundred readers specialised in all aspects of divination. Tarot cards, crystal ball, astrology, runes, messages from 'the other side', angel guidance. Sadie Chill, known as The Queen of Hearts liked power and her ego expanding with her bank balance she fired instantly any reader who opposed her. They gave her the nickname 'Cut-off-their-heads' and the turnover of staff was high. I asked how much Betty made, and the money was lamentable, the readers getting a fraction per minute of what the customer paid.

'If I ask for work what will they do?'

'Test you,' said Betty.

'What will they be looking for?'

'How long you keep the punter on line.'

I asked if there were any good readers, and she did mention several, especially Jade and Grey Owl, but they were always in demand. I needed a formula and asked which reader I could copy. She thought a straightforward tarot reader would be best and I should try Starlight.

I got her immediately, which was not a good sign, the ones who you queued for were worth the wait. She had a low soothing voice. 'I'm cutting a pack of cards into three. What shall I look for? Love? Home? Career?'

'Career.'

'Tell me what pack to use.'

'The first.'

'I'm spreading the cards in a circle. Shall I go clockwise?' This was taking too long. 'Will I get work as a singer?'

'The guides tell me of a red stone.'

She'd got my attention. 'Ruby Red' was my hit song. It had gone gold.

'It will take you through a new door, brightly painted.'

I remembered the Tunbridge Wells prediction. I hoped not that door. She talked about new songs and could see a contract. For now, adversity. She'd got that right.

'Watch for an Italian contact.' Her voice was changing, becoming hypnotic. It was decidedly an inviting sound that took my mind off everything else. A chime was struck and the reader with the amazing voice was gone. Not everything she'd said made any sense but she'd kept me from hanging up. Betty said they called that punter patter.

I was tested by Grey Owl and due to the 'cut-off-their-heads' regime there were spaces and I was taken on as a stand-in. It beat going back to stand-up in Camden Town. It was decided I had an attractive manner, was unlikely to be psychic but could stand up to stress. Stress? I'd sign my name on that line. Betty said they took me on because I sounded classy and could get the clients talking. Grey Owl gave me a pin number and the way to log on from my phone to the system. He added advice. 'Attune to the person's voice. What comes into your mind. Stick to money, love, luck. You work the busy shifts.' Before I even asked he said there was no negotiation on the money, so he probably could see what came next. I asked for a contract. Nothing like that. I'd work the general line and get paid for the minutes I was actually speaking.

'It's not bad, better than the sex lines. You don't need to advertise, hire a stall, tout for trade. The company do everything for you. All you do is pick up the phone in the comfort of your own home and your monthly pay cheque.'

The comfort of my home was non-existent as Ray for some inexplicable reason was adamantly against what he termed 'soothsayers'. He reminded me the local pub wanted a singer for the Sunday jazz band. My agent was trying to get me a tour of the Low Countries. I was lower than any country. It was better to do a different line of work for now. Ray treated me as though I'd become a criminal. 'It's fraudulent playing into people's dreams, giving false hope.' He was a reserve in the violins in a national orchestra, and on free nights played jazz in Camden. It was unlikely he'd be there during my on line hours. He couldn't believe what I was suggesting but then he'd only known me during the good times.

Betty taught me the routine. 'Shuffle a pack of cards and lay out 21. "2 red fours and aces red, a love bed", or "2 black knaves and a king, not a good thing". And you'd better get yourself believable credentials. They didn't go for the stuff you said about palm reading.'

I'd decided that was the only thing they couldn't test me on. Working a phone line I wouldn't see anyone's hand. They couldn't prove one way or another if I was a palm reader.

'Stick to tarot and copy the others,' said Betty.

'If I go wrong?'

'They'll disable your pin and take you off line. Don't let that happen. Good luck!'

And so I did get a new line of work. I became a telephone psychic.

CHAPTER 2

'MY NAME IS ISIS. Welcome to the Line. What's your name?'
The silence was due to nerves, uncertainty, or the caller wanted another reader. And then I understood it could be the sheep caller's husband so added some inducements. 'A female influence makes me see not a secret but a revelation.' I felt for Lou's messages hidden beside the phone. 'Let's ask what fate has in store for you.'

Nothing good, as it turned out, because Ray chose that moment to arrive unexpectedly and his exclamation unspiritual and penetrating could only have added to the caller's doubts.

'Alice Longbridge.' The caller had spoken. They rarely gave their second name. I could tell by her tone she was repressed and tricky, so used all the charm that I'd give a concert promoter and extracted her date of birth.

'She's lying.' Ray didn't bother to lower his voice. 'And I'm not even psychic.'

I asked if she'd like me to look at health or wealth at the same time flinging a handful of cutlery at my lover who ducked and it hit the wall and clattered across the floor. The noise might be explained as a psychic presence if not for Ray's laugh, an only too earthly sound.

'The spirits are certainly here tonight,' he shouted. Was he drunk? I hurled a teapot, and its contents made an interesting challenge to the bland wallpaper and was more in keeping with the new career trying to take place in the room. I would lose Mrs Longbridge. She'd hang up and report me and what I dreaded most, my pin number disabled would cut off the rest of my calls. The woman took no notice of this unusual activity and was there for the duration, domestic, psychic. I quickly offered her again the usual choice of fortune but Mrs Longbridge said, 'I don't want any of that.' And then she reminded me of a long forgotten neighbour tight-laced, malicious, church-going, Welsh. Something in this caller's voice brought back the neighbour's presence, bad body in prim clothes filling the doorway. She wanted trouble, others' downfall, but covered it with a crust of goodness, all shallow and pious, the sort her church liked. I couldn't recall her name. Remembering that woman helped me tune in to this caller and I understood from the past what I was dealing with in the present. Spite. The woman wanted power over me just as the neighbour had over everyone.

'I want to help you, Mrs Longbridge.' I was thinking of the neighbour.

'Help me? You're a fraud. I gave you a false name and date of birth and you didn't even know it.'

Dreading poverty, I must not lose Mrs Longbridge, I must not lose this job. Keep the punter on the line. Ace up the sleeve. I moved my new How to Read Tarot Cards book to one side and rested both elbows on the table. This needed attention. This could be the quality control test I'd heard about. All new readers got it.

'Whatever your name, your feelings are the same. I sense you're lonely. I can see a box. Is it photographs from the past?' That was a long shot, but as I talked to her I did see a box. Everyone had a box. Admittedly it was in my mind but it didn't give a pleasant feeling.

'An old dodge,' said Ray. 'The old man's dole. She calls it

housekeeping. You'll find it under the photographs.' Drink certainly had a part to play but clairvoyance brought out the worst in him. How I hoped the management was not listening in. 'Lonely' had triggered a new Mrs Longbridge. Furious, she said, 'Of course I'm lonely. He's dead, isn't he, but you don't know how . . .'

'Your husband?'

'He's not far away but you don't see him and . . .' She was swept away and the line was empty.

I sat, holding the phone. I could actually see a box of ashes on the chair opposite her. She kept him there. The movie Psycho didn't cover all the territory. Eyes shut I could see the chair, his chair and in it a rotting corpse and on the thigh bones balanced a box, lid lifted, that got my eyes open. The corpse faded, leaving the box of ashes now closed. Was this clairvoyance?

Ray didn't wait for the attack that would come next. Quite sober, he said, 'I just can't bear to see you doing this. I . . .' He couldn't continue and the phone rang and he said to leave it. And get logged off? Not a chance. I suspected he felt guilty he wasn't taking on the money problem and looking after me. I hadn't thought of that before. I asked the woman's date of birth and, catching sight of the splashed tea on the virgin wall brought on a moment of near hysteria. I had to fight off terrible laughter. The tea had formed a pattern which wasn't without point. From rage came this surge of delicate droplets that could be interpreted as unshed tears. A whole tsunami of suppressed grief rising in this substantial wave was stamped indelibly like a psychic logo. Was this my guide? Still rocking with laughter, I managed to give the woman one of Betty's predictions, a sure thing that usually never failed. The caller hung up.

Ray didn't lose any time and said my transformation to soothsayer was beyond anything a psychic could think up and I thought he was actually going to pull the phone from the socket. Then he surprised me. This would be my last session as he'd got me a job replacing a singer at a good venue for seven nights. I didn't like the 'replacing' but I'd take the job. He'd negotiate the money and bring in the necessary people, even a new agent. It would kick-start my career.

The phone rang more quickly than usual and the woman said her name and date of birth immediately, so she was a regular. I gave her the choice and added children. She laughed maliciously and for a moment I was sure it was Mrs Longbridge. I could see not the box of ashes now but her husband alive in the chair wearing a hand-knitted pullover. I knew he was too thin and rigid and on the verge of becoming very ill. They'd done the operation but not got everything. They'd told him he was bound to feel unwell after the operation but must look on the bright side. I felt sad and looked at the wave of psychic tears on the wall to cheer me up. How did I know all this? Of course it was some memory from my own childhood.

'I don't want any of that.' Prim now, she was the grey-haired neighbour from my past.

'What do you want?'

The news about the job gave me strength to fight back.

'I want to know about my guardian angel.'

'What on earth for?' I was really surprised. Who would want to know about angels at one pound fifty a minute?

'I want to know who's around me?'

'Why?'

'I'm curious. Why shouldn't I be?' She was contentious now in a small way.

I didn't know one angel from the next. Guardian angels? Did they have names?

'Archangel Michael,' said Ray. 'They always like him. Top of the heap.'

The woman couldn't miss the intrusion but stayed on the line.

'Who else?' she added, sharp as an ace of swords.

Ray laughed. 'She's greedy for angels.'

'You don't need anyone else if you've got the archangel.' I nearly called her Mrs Longbridge. 'What do you want to know from the angel?'

'What can it see around me?'

The automated voice, announcing the two minutes remaining, cut in.

'You don't know a thing. You're rubbish.' The neighbour from the past was back in the doorway with her pebbledash white walls, too neat garden. You sit in your call centre and you'll never get me . . .' If the sentence ever continued I would not have known because the call was cut.

'She thinks this is a call centre,' I told Ray. 'But you can't go on intruding or I can't do it.'

'But you don't have to.'

She phoned twice more her voice disguised but not enough. She wanted to know if it was possible to detect what was opposite her in that chair. I was sure of it. Could a psychic? Better still, a guardian angel. Would her crime go undetected?

'How do you know she did him in?' said Ray. 'Perhaps she couldn't bear to be left so she's kept his ashes. It might not be a husband. Could be her dog.'

I repeated what I could of her boastful jibes.

'She's crazy. It's obvious,' he said, 'why tell you?'

'To see if it's detectable. Will she get found out?'

I was glad the next caller only wanted her husband back.

CHAPTER 3

I DID THE GIG and then four nights at Jazz Café. As soon as I got home I worked the late shift for 5p a minute extra. This was a different class of caller. Drugs and drink came into it, desperation, sexual banter, insults, reckless spending on repeat calls and cut off on mobile phones. 'Will he come back? Will she come back? I've only credit for one question.' I didn't need to go to a psychic with my question – my career was not resuscitated.

Betty, again, concerned about the short duration of my calls, phoned with advice. 'A hang-up is noticed, too many fatal. Remember always have that ace up your sleeve. Make the punter feel good.'

I made it clear when I worked Ray could not be there and he didn't like it. 'First you lose your career. Then your guy. And on top you get obsessed with fortune-telling.'

Obsessed? Terrified more like it. I must not lose this line. Now I actually tried to face the financial reality that I'd spent months escaping I saw the debt as a mountain, its summit out of sight, untouchable. I couldn't even do the interest. That couldn't even be approached by the psychic earnings.

I told Ray the same as I told myself. This was very short-term but at least it put the breakfast on the table. He got the drift of fear, unusual in me, and said he'd do what he could to find another gig. He was looking at me as though he'd never seen my face like this. Did I suddenly look old? 'Get fresh air,' he said, and left for his own place.

5 a.m., and I sat waiting for the next call. I'd wait till dawn came up and then go out on Primrose Hill and get the air he talked about. I must negotiate an even bigger loan. I should heave myself up into a new show and tour it round the UK. Get the songs on CD. One more try. I owed myself that much.

✳

I still expected the call from the sheep husband and realised I didn't know his name or date of birth. I needed information, something to work on and asked Betty if she could check Lou out with other readers. It had been over three weeks since that second call. Betty got through to Sadie Chill's assistant, Riff, and found that the woman I knew as Lou had phoned three others before me for less than six minutes each. 'She's only come on recently and no one remembers her. Riff tracked her details from her mobile booking with you.'

How?'

'They've got a data base. All calls recorded.'

I was appalled.

'They have to in case they're sued. He tracked her easily because she was your first reading. Even Grey Owl got a hang-up from her. He's too good for her obviously. She uses a different name and birth date each time but the same mobile number.'

'He's too good for her.' That stayed with me. How bad was I? I had no psychic ability, look how I'd ended up. Betty promised me everyone had some extra sense, but how did I find it?

'Link with the caller. Stick to the cards. An ace and two fours, red, a love bed.'

Who'd believe that? People who want to believe there's a better future, those who need a better present. She promised me they'd go for anything. Two fours red, a love bed? No problem there. For her.

I decided on another direction and took tarot card readings by phone with Grey Owl, his fee to come out of my monthly payment. I could do a Celtic cross, which indicated past, present and outcome and it gave me confidence with those phone strangers. The cards took the responsibility. I felt I could link with women easier, especially those who didn't have what they most wanted. Some still hung up in the middle of one of my predictions without saying anything and gave a good lesson in handling rejection. Occasionally, after a full twenty minutes live line call the person rang back and I felt I'd done something of value. Ray did not and disliked the giving of false hope. He said I was faking it, that it was fake. I reminded him of the bunch of unpaid bills. On a good night I made £50, but I was hanging on by luck.

'Let's do the UK tour,' he said, and made an appointment with the bank for the following week. 'Start writing the material and I'll get a recording studio.'

He wanted me to promise I'd get off line and in its place he'd rent out his flat, do extra concerts, and take out a loan. No, he did not like fake.

I was grateful and could see I did mean something to him, it hadn't just been the good times, but the trouble was when he was absent I went back on line. It could be fear, a need for security, or these days the flat seemed empty and me with it.

When I next spoke to Betty I asked how long she'd been on the line and she'd started it as a way to pay off her car which would take six months. Six years later she worked even longer hours. 'It sort of gets you, becomes a habit. It's easy. But you need regular callers and keep hold of them. Grey Owl and Jade can have the same callers every night.'

I asked about 'Fake' and 'False Hope' and she didn't see it as a moral issue.

'There are thirty on line at any given time and some just make everything up, but in the end don't do business and get weeded out. Others use text book techniques. Most are a mixture of authentic and sham. There are good sensitive readers and they attune to the energies and information around a client. They don't give false anything but if they see something bad they know how to let the client down lightly. It should be a healing process, not a shock.' She suddenly stopped and I thought we were cut off. Then she said, 'Just listen. Let them talk. That might work with you.' Another pause. 'People are lonely.

CHAPTER 4

AND THEN I GOT the call. The man was educated, sophisticated and I knew it was him. I didn't have to be psychic to know that. He was foreign born in 1966 which I now knew made him a fire-horse in Chinese astrology, the worst sign for anyone. Luckily it only came around every sixty years. Having recently read about the fire-horse in the astrology manual, I felt quite confident telling him his emotional life was a rollercoaster and he didn't disagree. I asked who'd told him to use the line and he became defensive. I was trying to confirm Lou's participation in this. What did he want? I gave him the usual choice. He said messages. From whom? Just to be sure.

'You tell me. You're the psychic.'

I told him about his guide and that there were messages from the world of spirit.

'O.K.' He seemed to agree.

I got the list from under the phone and read as though receiving them from another place. I thanked the spirits that Ray wasn't in the room.

'O.K. that's enough.'

Surprised I said, 'But she wanted you to hear all of it.'

'She?'

Slip up. Backtrack. 'I told you. The guide.'
'If you don't mind I will conclude this reading.'
'But I haven't finished.'
'You make no sense.'
'But this is a message from spirit.' I must stop him from hanging up. 'Does it upset you?'
'It means absolutely nothing to me.' And he was gone.

✻

I sat on Primrose Hill looking out across London and wondered what Lou was trying to obtain by the messages. The focus seemed to be on generosity of spirit, getting the man to see the bigger picture. We don't take it with us when we go and we don't go on forever. Why had I believed so instantly that this was the voice of the husband who needed to believe in better things? Because he was a cut above the usual caller. Because he fitted with her. Why had the call taken so long? She had to persuade him to call me, or she'd thought twice about the whole thing. I remembered her voice and hoped I'd hear it again.

The bank manager was not impressed with the first month's payment from the line but I wasn't in his office for approval. I asked to increase the loan. It might be the Mt Everest of loans but on optimistic days you could still see the summit. I'd made this sudden appointment at the bank, without Ray, without waiting for the one we had the following week because I needed to know, and privately, how things stood. I found out and would have left the bank in tears if I had any inside me. I wasn't a weeping person by nature. Laughter, even the cynical kind, was my release. Maybe the surge of tears on my wall did my crying for me. Next into the agent's office, another impulsive visit with no better outcome.

Back on Primrose Hill, I questioned the very idea of clairvoyance. Was it fake, a way to cheer people up, to give them a sense of importance? They could be lonely as Betty suggested.

Perhaps a clairvoyant was the only person they spoke to all week. I realised I was looking at a tree, its early spring leaves just visible. I was quite relaxed, just taking it in and if I could let go I may be able to attune to the tree. And then, if I became focused, I could absorb information I wouldn't normally receive. Wasn't that what Grey Owl had described? I felt something did change and I was aware of the tree in a different way, finding it had a slight atmosphere of its own, a resonance. For a moment I linked with it. It was as simple as that. Was this clairvoyance? For a few minutes I felt completely absorbed by this tree to the exclusion of everything else.

Cheered up, I hurried home actually looking forward to receiving calls and going deeper into the subject. Would my attuning experience on Primrose Hill take me into other realities? First I spoke with Grey Owl and he gave me another speciality to assist with 'seeing'. Opening and closing the Chakras. There were seven from the base of the spine to the crown of the head. By visualising each one in colour I could cause a change in their activity. I knew some of this from yoga practice and meditation. He then told me how to wrap myself in a sheath of golden light from the top of my head down to the soles of my feet. This was to protect me and my growing sensitivity.

'In times of danger use a green triangle or pyramid. See it covering the assailant. Mid-green. Just pop it over the person thus keeping their negativity inside and away from you using an ancient Egyptian symbol. In a dangerous crisis visualise a number 3 in mid-green over the solar plexus of the assailant. Give the number 3 a long curving tail.'

I thanked him and said I hoped I wouldn't need it.

'And when you're on line never give a person their date of death.'

I should be so lucky.

I replaced the receiver and got a call immediately. A young man asked if the woman he was with could be considered honest.

'In what way?'

'You tell me.' He had a slight accent probably from Liverpool.

Could this be 'the husband'?

'In love matters, yes.' I had no idea.

'What if you're not seeing straight?' Not Lou's husband, definitely. Too common.

'I'm seeing that if she feels love like anyone else she'll honestly recognise that feeling.' That got rid of him. Not quite.

'What if she betrays him, Miss Sit-on-the-fence?'

'I don't think I'm tuning into you.'

'At least that's honest.'

'Hang up and get another reader.'

He laughed. 'Honest or not? Shall I trust her?'

'Why don't you trust yourself? Your own judgement?'

'What does she think of me?

'That you're sometimes opinionated. Even smug.' I had no idea about her but I wanted him off the line.

'So I should trust her?'

'I didn't say that.'

'You shouldn't be on line.'

This one would lose me the job. This was the pin disabler. The answer I wanted to give would be forever silent. Instead I must appease this pest.

He said, 'So you're not honest.' And he laughed and hung up.

I logged off, considered phoning the readers' support line. Instead I went back to Primrose Hill, it was the one place I loved, and here I could be honest.

And then I realised who I'd had on line. I phoned Ray and asked what the hell he was doing. He laughed. 'Just testing you.'

'At one fifty a minute.'

'It was worth it. And my dialect wasn't bad.'

Of course he'd sounded not unfamiliar now I thought about it. The rhythm of his speech, the communicative intent. Should I tell him about the impulsive trip to the bank?

'You're not going to give up, are you?'

I said I'd give it one more week. Should I mention Betty's conclusion that I was dealing with the lonely. He said he was getting extra money by standing in for another musician on tour. He'd be back by the weekend.

'We keep that appointment with the bank manager on Tuesday, and then you stop.' He waited.

'Agreed?'

I agreed.

'Honest?'

For now. One thing about his psychic line call: I hadn't realised how young he sounded. I hadn't realised how young he actually was.

CHAPTER 5

TO WORK THE LINE the reader needed a stable phone with no answer message, preferably hands free. I had a stable phone but the other two requirements were not in place. I wouldn't be doing this long enough. To connect to the system I had to log on using a personal pin number, next a security code and then hang up and wait for calls to be put through. Beside me a glass of fresh water, a pen, paper to record the date and reader's name and duration of call. In front of me a clock with a large face and two packs of tarot cards. I lifted the receiver with some expectation. It was better now Ray was not there. This session would be different. I wasn't wrong about that. Maybe I was getting clairvoyant? The pin did not register. Had Ray done something? I tried again then rang BT. I was due on at six and now fifteen minutes late. I got through to Riff and heard the terrible word 'disabled'. My pin was withheld. This was the beginning of a bad illness. The first symptom left me confused, and then I couldn't believe it. Even they made mistakes. My mouth was dry as I waited for some explanation.

'You're off line until further notice.'

A surge of cold fear made its way up my now identifiable chakras. What had I done? He said yesterday's caller had made no sense of the messages, had complained and wanted his money back. I defended myself fiercely and asked to speak to Sadie Chill.

'Not until she listens to the recording. Only she makes the decision.'

'So you do record all the readings?' I hadn't really believed it, thinking it must be a way to keep the readers sharp.

'Every word. In case of legal action. The company is vulnerable. Your calls are dated and logged in the usual way.'

'Can I go on working until you listen to the recording?'

He said that wasn't allowed and I'd have to wait. I asked how long and he had no idea.

'Please, don't hang up.'

He hung up.

I slumped onto the chair, bereft, realising how fixed I was on the line. It was my life line. I needed the phone to ring, the caller to speak, the minutes to tick by at 35p each one, taking me on the journey into other lives. Then I was furious. How could the company do this to me? Didn't they know who I was? Sweating, heart fluttering, I asked for Sadie.

'We're looking into it,' Riff sighed.

'This won't do,' I shouted.

Riff hung up.

I couldn't bear the silence, Ray away on tour, I couldn't reach my agent. I sat for a long time waiting, the amputation severe. This was a definite withdrawal from a link I needed. I was no longer sure it was just the money. It had taken just six weeks to be this dependent.

I got Betty eventually and she said it was one of their ways of getting rid of someone, using a phoney complaint so I asked what she could do. She said she couldn't get into this as her own status was too precarious.

'They've got a preferred handful and now a new chick on line who's supposed to be shit-hot. Sue Ann. She can even get names like your boyfriend, your mother. But they won't keep her because the money's not attractive enough. They've got her doing turns in a London hairdresser's. Now you've got to get yourself up to scratch. You've told them you're a palm reader. Better know something about it. The lines on the palm mean something. Going across the top is the emotional line, the one beneath the head line. The lifeline runs in a curve around the mount below the thumb. The destiny line runs down the palm to the wrist. Remember the mounts: Venus, Jupiter, the moon, and the sun lines under the ring finger; length of fingers short, long, how they relate to each other, and their flexibility. It all forms a picture of the person's past and future. Don't forget the bracelets. They're lines around the wrists. You look for a star, a trine, a cross. An island is bad news.'

I thanked her and she asked what I thought of being a phone psychic. It wasn't mystical as I'd thought. The callers were only too real.

Throughout that desolate evening I tried to phone Sadie, Riff and the support manager Howard, who was supposed to look after the readers, even the disabled ones. How had this happened? Perhaps I should phone the psychic line. I phoned the local pub and asked about the Sunday jazz singing vacancy. The manager at first couldn't believe it was me. He was amazed that I should even consider it.

'We couldn't go near what you make. It's an honour Jesse. I was playing "Ruby Red" the other night. Amazing. It's a joke, isn't it, you're working for us?'

I agreed it was. Obviously my career crash had not reached the pub circuit. I tried to laugh it off. I couldn't laugh off my singing teacher's outstanding bill and had to put voice work on hold for now. He was one of the best and my slot would be taken. What had happened? Wasn't I a telephone psychic? Shouldn't I know? At 1 a.m. Riff called to say they'd listened to the recording and the messages sounded like instructions.

'How do I know? I can't criticise the spirit that speaks through me.'

I could tell Riff didn't believe it, any of it, even if it came from shit-hot Sue Ann. I considered telling this arrogant upstart, my real name. And then let them see what they missed. Of course I would log off for good. He told me Sadie would call later and I should get some sleep.

I walked to and fro the small flat feeling a strange but definite withdrawal from a link I must need. It wasn't just the money. I'd lost over £50 during this hellish night, but I used to make ten times that on a gig after the show and how it got spent I would never know or care.

✳

Sadie Chill phoned the following afternoon sounding quite cheerful and said I was popular. A client had tried half the night to reach me so I could stay on line for now but my calls would be monitored daily.

'Who was the client?'

'A woman.'

I asked who. I had the feeling it was Lou.

'Never mind her name. Just say your guardian angel because she's kept you working. It would have been the chop, Isis. If you get another caller you can't link with suggest another reader.' She was intrigued by the messages. What were they/ Of course it would be Lou who had saved me.

Now I was angry and wanted to quit. How could I be put through something so brutal which had caused such havoc in me? I looked through Variety and other job sheets, told my agent I'd do backing singer, the Low Countries were not as low as they were. TV jingles? Count me in.

Betty on next with advice. 'You have to connect with the caller and increase the call duration otherwise they'll keep you on graveyard shift. You must make the punter feel he or she is the most important person in the world. Concentrate on them utterly. Make them feel great. Keep the speed up. Keeping saying something important is about to come through. Remember the management always listens in to newcomers' calls. Make sure you get on the credit card line. That's the elite. The client books you for a set time and you get a higher rate. Aim for that.'

This was all bad news and, determined to keep the next reader for the full twenty minutes, I talked non-stop and suspected I sounded crazy. Ray's expression confirmed that. I went on at full speed until the automatic 'two minutes left' signal came on and the woman got free of me. Ray asked if I was on something and, foolishly, I told him about Betty's advice. Knowing his attitude, I had decided never to share anything about the line again.

'So I give it all I've got,' I concluded.

'Just like any whore.'

I asked where that came from exactly.

'A good working girl makes the guy feel great. He's the most important dude in the world, shit-hot at everything and they haven't even been in the sack yet.'

Just back from the short tour he put two bags of groceries on the table and said he'd make dinner. The phone rang and I shuffled the pack.

'Another hostage,' he sighed.

This one talked more than I did. She cut through every sparkling optimistic sentence I started and told me about two deaths, illness, mortgage problems and noisy neighbours. Was she unlucky? she asked. If Ray hadn't been in the next room I'd have used the never to be forgiven and ridiculed for all time word Karma. Ray would have got his teeth into that, he'd put it on my grave. The line took the woman away just as it had brought her in.

Howard, the reader's support manager, came on next, asking how I'd handled the previous caller. I said I couldn't relate to her. Whatever I said she didn't listen. She had just talked and talked and he said she was always like that and I should learn when to speak and when to listen.

I realised it didn't matter. Most just wanted to know one thing: am I loved?

'What about the jazz session at the pub?' Ray pulled some papers from his bag.

Never. I'd sooner do backing singer. The papers became a fistful of bills and he presented them with a flourish. It used to be roses. Backing singer it is. Could it get worse? It could. There were no backing singer jobs. Next came the dole.

'Welcome to the Line. My name's Isis.'

CHAPTER 6

ANOTHER HOUR TICKED BY noisily on the big-faced clock and when the phone did ring I jumped to pick it up, hands all over it as though trying to catch an escaping pet. Sadie Chill was well named and the first sound of her sent my temperature dropping. I did a lot of 'cold' these days.

'I'm still listening to your readings and you've got to go further.' She talked about getting in touch with other realms. 'Do you know "the edge"?'

What else? But I didn't tell her.

'Have you been there?'

'Definitely.'

She hesitated. 'Then tell them that. Speak to them from the edge.'

I realised they were having to reinvent me. 'The Edge'. I wasn't doing too good in the middle.

The next call introduced me to the elitist credit line. This was a reading pre-booked for 45 minutes. Riff would put me through and he said to watch the introduction. I had to be sharp.

I didn't recognise Mrs Sheep until she said: 'So, how did we do with my husband? Has he been converted?'

Had I had her husband? I sped through the male callers of the past days, trying to recall each one. Had I missed him? The only

candidate was the one born in 1966 who'd nearly cost me my job.
'So he hasn't been on line? Where is he d'you think, Isis?'
I had no idea where anybody was.
'Maybe he's hiding in the sheep croft.' Lou liked to laugh.
Mindful of the fact she might be my guardian angel and had
saved my job for now, I did ask if she'd tried to reach me one
night the previous week while I'd been off the air.
'As a matter of fact I wanted you to read for a friend and was
surprised you were, as you put it, off the air. You're always on.'
How did she know that? Did she check through customer
services? I asked for her date of birth and prepared to take
control of this reading and fill it up somehow.
'You have such a thrilling voice. You're so good, Isis. Anyone
would believe you. I am also giving you my brother. Now I will
give you a few markers for him. Write them down.'
She was used to getting her way. I tried to get both men's
names and dates of birth, but she asked me to read the original
messages for her husband. She was checking I still had them.
'We don't need names, Isis. Everyone in this business changes
them anyway.' She laughed. Was she thinking of mine? She
asked me to speak a little more slowly as though listening to the
message. 'Don't read it. Hear it.'
'Why is it so important?'
'Why indeed. We both want a better world, don't we, Isis?'
I told her according to her birth date she, under the sign of
Libra, wanted to make a spiritual balance.
'Drop all that. Just give your best performance.'
How had she chosen that word? Maybe she should be the psychic.

*

Was it insecurity that produced the dream? I could see wheels
coming towards me and if I ran across the road I'd just get
away. But she grabbed me with a possessiveness that was more
compelling than approaching death. The wheels were too near.

I heard the sound of a body hitting the ground, the scream, and then I turned to accept the carnage. I saw the small thing rolling slowly towards the kerb. I bent to look at it. It was an eyeball. It was enough to wake me up in a good sweat, heart pounding. What happened to her? Of course I knew her but she faded, without identification, away with the dream.

'Tell me.' Ray was awake.

And then I couldn't remember. I hadn't had it for years, not since I was a child.

At the Tuesday meeting, the bank manager, the stuff of bad dreams, sat safe behind the big desk while I described the solution for the loan. I'd compose new material, put out a CD and tour the UK. I'd go back to the voice teacher. I'd give it everything, all bets off, one last try. I'd also do some of the old ballads. I owed it to myself.

He said we'd had this discussion last week and his answer hadn't changed. I assured him that the previous week I'd asked simply for a loan. Now it was a solution. I'd asked Ray to wait outside and make a second attempt if necessary.

I thought the bank manager would ask what had gone wrong but he was more interested in what had gone wrong in his bank. My accounts. He chose the word 'excessive'. I said that might be the case but the line earnings wouldn't do much to change that adjective. He asked what increase I was looking for and following Ray's advice I made it large enough. He said he'd have to consider my request. I brought Ray in for his turn but the bank manager was as closed as some of the callers I had to divine for on line. Afterwards, Ray said I was always an optimist. I thought gambler might be the term these days. I didn't get the loan increase and tried other banks. Then I was offered a summer show on the pier at Worthing. I got several days backing singer. My song 'Ruby Red' would be released in a mixed album. I'd only need to shuffle the cards one more month.

✳

I did the usual introduction and Mrs Longbridge spent the full twenty minutes relieving herself of spite, malice and life's disappointments. Dumping it on a stranger gave her a necessary satisfaction, but not any stranger. She needed me. I was the almost perfect foil. All I had to do was activate the memory of the neighbour in the past and I could come up with responses made for the reading. 'Fraud' still reverberating through the phone wall to wall like small darts of lightning was her last insult before cut-off. The phone rang immediately and I thought dissatisfied she was calling back for more.

The man was gentle with a measured voice and I dropped the edgy tone that would have met Mrs Longbridge. He was from the Middle East, educated, professional, and I switched to soft-spoken, affirming, optimistic all-seeing adviser as I tried to get the sheets of notes in front of me without rustling the paper. This was 'the husband'.

As I read Lou's words it seemed the spirit world wanted this man to give to Lou what was Lou's and this would be his amend to her. He would be repaid a thousand times.

'Can you repeat that please?'

I changed it to a dozen.

'So where are you getting all this from?'

'From the spiritual guides linking with us.'

He seemed unsure and asked again about guides and their purpose. I tried to remember Grey Owl's teaching to give clarity to their existence.

'What happens if I don't follow their guidance?'

The problem was Lou had only written my part of the script. She hadn't considered his replies or questions. I was careful to tell him that nothing would happen. I didn't want a possible blackmail angle on top of everything else. 'You just miss the spirit's repayment.'

He thanked me and hung up. He was not convinced, not by any of it. I didn't have time to consider my predicament because Sarah Chill came on next.

'Why do you keep coming out with this stuff? It sounds as though you don't know what to say, so read him these instructions. Yes, we are listening in, Isis.'

I nearly said this instruction reading had cost me a night's work, but saying that would lose me my job.

'Are they messages?' Her voice chilled, she was well named.

'Just from the edge.'

She hung up, another not convinced by my skill.

Ray came in with a selection of newspapers and magazines open at the horoscope page. 'Stick with that and you can't go wrong.' Seeing I was determined to stay on another month, he kept his objections to himself. I felt the grim answer from the bank had made 'soothsayers' a little more tolerable. Ray still believed my career would be back on course and that the CD we planned would take off.

'It's not the time to get a new agent but the minute you hit the yellow brick road again kick that sleeper out. And don't lose sleep about that loan. The manager's full of pig-shit. They'll have to write it off.'

Ray was nine years younger than me and had his tough side. Music was his life and I was no clairvoyant, but I couldn't see him hit the wall as I had. What had gone wrong? I couldn't bear the post-mortem. I made sure I spent an hour a day on voice work and twice a week in the gym. It only took one phone call to change my life and I had to be prepared.

Finally, I had a formula for the work on line: name, date of birth, had they been on line before? They often said no, believing they'd get a better reading as a tarot virgin. I immediately looked for something in the caller's attitude that I understood, a quality that reminded me of someone from my past. Using that memory I could tune into a fact or character trait that fitted the present caller. Sometimes. At others, hang up. It was my way of being psychic and I was no longer nervous. After all I'd had Tunbridge Wells and the red door. How could I disprove it? It was all in the future. That reader had simply used a technique and given me a performance. I'd do the same. First I used tarot cards and let the reader say when I should stop shuffling and how to cut the pack. And now I added astrology from a tabloid. I was a mongrel reader, made up of bits of Betty, Starlight and Tunbridge Wells. Did the company still listen in? They couldn't have listened to Lou's bookings or they'd have known where the messages came from.

When he wasn't working Ray came round to play cards. He listened as I got another twenty minutes call, and another, dragging up energy, doing a performance, not letting them have any gaps for their own quite often hostile reactions. Ray listened, not without a certain fascination.

'If you go on yapping to the caller like that they'll have you on the sex line.' He reheated my unfinished dinner. 'If you're going to stick with this . . .'

'Which I'm not . . .'

'Be smart and get the callers to have a personal reading. Get them away from the company. Charge properly because they're getting it one to one.'

'So you see some benefit doing this?' I said.

'No one knows you're doing it. And Worthing is less than a month away.' He paused. 'You really try and I admire you for that.'

The phone rang and he picked up the receiver and gave it to me. This call didn't have the usual greeting. Sadie Chill said, 'Never, ever meet a customer or read for them out of hours. We'll take you off line immediately and give you no protection.'

My blood went cold as it seemed to do in this job. After the touch of 'off with your head', she said, 'You work for spirit and let spirit work through you.' Did she believe this stuff? 'Have I made myself clear, Isis?'

Definitely. Ray mentions ripping off the customers one minute and she's on the line the next. Either she was a psychic or she had my room bugged.

*

Although I'd logged on at 10 p.m. I waited an hour for the first call, not without certain desperation. I did not like the waiting. Was I, like the old-timers, hooked? I seemed to sink into this night world of contact with people I'd never meet, making sense of their dreams, their pain. The night lent the contact a certain mystery which could not exist in daylight. For the first time I had to know another person simply by their voice. I was rehearsing the Daily Mail predictions when the caller gave her name and date of birth.

'You don't know anything about me.' Mrs Longbridge sounded coy. 'You can't even tell what I'm thinking.'

I was thinking could Mrs Longbridge afford this? She averaged twenty minutes, costing £30 a night just with me. How was I supposed to protect her at the bank? She laughed, not the most pleasant sound I'd heard.

'Do you people talk to dead ones?' A common touch now. I wasn't sure anymore it was Mrs Longbridge.

'If those in spirit want to communicate they will approach.' One of Sadie's lines that couldn't go wrong.

'Has he left me money?'

She waited and I could hear her breath.

'So look for it in a three.' Tunbridge Wells confidence kicking in. Yes, the red front door had had a gold knocker, obviously gilt.

I didn't expect Lou so soon and I did not want to admit her husband had not been convinced by my performance. Again she had booked a credit call and again I didn't know how to fill this forty-five minutes slot. She asked if I'd had many credit readings and I said she had been the first.

'And your first client on the live line. You are my psychic virgin.' She didn't bother with the laugh this time and sounded – was it enticing? Alert now, I asked how she knew she was the first.

'Because you've never been on before. I checked with the sales team.'

'Why?'

'What a lot of questions, Isis.' Enticing moment over.

But not 'the question!' I should be asking if she knew her husband had been on line. This was the time to say it.

'You are supposed to give answers, Isis, before I've asked questions. That's what a psychic does.'

She'd had servants and knew how to get what she paid for. I felt reduced as though I was dusting the corner of a room. My God, did that come next?

'You are stubborn, Isis, and if you weren't so delicious you'd never get away with it.'

And I got it. She was trying to get me for a threesome with the husband. I told her firmly that born under Libra this month would be plagued with delays caused by Mercury in retrograde – and the moon was going through an eclipse and . . .'

'Drop all that.'

Had she heard the newspaper rustle?

'I'll always call on the credit line, Isis. It will give you more money.'

I said that wasn't necessary.

'Surely you don't take a snooty attitude towards money?'

I thought we were becoming too personal but remembered she had saved my job. Now I must tell her about the husband's call. Another question and it would be too late. If I told her now she'd say why hadn't I said so at the beginning. I would then say why didn't she ask. Thirty-five minutes to go but she, however, was not going to waste a moment. Her voice slowed and became undeniably seductive. If a sound was charismatic this was it. Her voice was strangely not unfamiliar and I felt I'd known her all my life.

'Why don't you speak, Isis?' She was tempting me and next I'd be a schoolgirl with a crush. Of all the penalties this work offered I could never have dreamt this.

'They've put a photograph of you on their magazine ads. It's not you, is it? It's a library photograph.'

I had no idea, not having seen it.

'Are you born under the sign Pisces?'

'Some days.'

That made her laugh.

'You will do everything I ask, won't you?'

And I could feel the voice in every nerve stirring like a man making love to me. Who was this woman? I had to watch it. Not only the guides listened in.

'Work on him, Isis, and when he rings be young and sweet and tell him each thing in order.'

'Lou, your guide, is aware of this conversation. And so are other guides, more human – that's what I pick up.'

If she picked up my warning she didn't care. 'You have the sheets of instructions by your phone, don't you? Keep them nearby. You will be well cared for. I'm going to hang up now.'

I was appalled. 'But you've only been on fifteen minutes.'

'Don't worry. You'll still be paid for the full booking. Love you.' And the voice was swept away, and I was left with a feeling I'd find hard to define.

For a moment I'd thought I was alone with her. Of course, Howard, Riff and icy Miss Chill were also listening. Were they laughing? Mocking? The new reader getting the treatment from a determined female. Not only was she turning psychic but possibly gay.

CHAPTER 7

'I'M STARLIGHT AND I know you're going off line.' It was
2.20 a.m. 'Give me a number I can call.' Hers was a night-time
voice and I asked if she'd been a performer.

'Just give me the number.' When she rang back she said the
company often listened in. She didn't think I'd last as a psychic
and had a proposition which might work better. A new line
was being set up and she would be in charge of the readers. We
arranged to meet in Camden Lock the next day and I asked how
I'd recognise her.

'Pink and mauve silk chiffon dress. Black hair. Green eyes.
And you?'

I was less glorious.

She was a shock because she was nothing like the voice.
Colour-blind too. Green? The eyes were brown. Her head was
oddly misshapen, too long at the top. The eyes met close over a
nose too large and long. The eyebrows were dark and thick and
ran uninterrupted in a primitive line across the brow. She had
a beautiful mouth and enviable teeth and a superb body but
somehow you saw all that too late.

She recognised me from my CDs, and her expression was
assessing and sharp and didn't belong to the rest of her. For a

moment she held both my hands in hers. 'It happened suddenly,' she said. 'I'm sorry for you.' She meant my career flop. 'Styles change but what I am going to offer you doesn't.' She let our hands part and we walked along the canal as she described a new chat line for which she was getting readers. 'I've picked you, Jesse, because you have a good vocal approach and a lot of atmosphere. And you're quick and on top of the material.'

'But not psychic.'

'No problem with that one. Not for this line.'

'Where's the money coming from?' These days I kept my feet on the ground.

'I've got funding.'

'How much are you paying?'

'Eighteen pence a minute, to start.'

That figure was familiar. 'Isn't that the sex line rate?'

'Exactly. That's what this is, but classier than the others. Your rate per minute will double within a month and triple after that. We guarantee you to . . .'

'I can't do that.' I actually laughed. The thought of what I'd be trying to do made seeing the future almost easy. She assured me the rate doubled again if I included SM. She'd left reality and was giving me spin no one would believe. Briefly, I said this service was not something I would contemplate. I imagined Ray appearing unexpectedly during one of these calls.

'Haven't you done phone sex?'

I said her offer was not for me and I wished her luck. So she gave me a pay rise that if it had been factual would have sorted out the clouds at the summit of debt mountain. She said she would use the prudent business reserve to cover my salary.

'It's just that I think you'd be really good.'

I knew why she wanted me. I had been successful and sought after, and that would be used to advantage promoting that line. She'd discreetly let some of the clients know who was giving them the treatment. Again, I said no.

'You don't even have to think. You just read the script. That's what sex lines are. Radio plays.'

I asked who wrote them and hoped for the caller's sake it wasn't her. She was very proud to bring in Paul Raymond Productions.

'You have heard of Raymond Revues Bar. He writes all the scripts.'

I wasn't sure he was still around in any sense, but was interested how this ugly beautiful person could set up a company. 'So you have to quickly find the script for the particular type of caller.'

'Exactly.'

'How long is the reading?'

'Like Sadie, I'll do twenty minutes, but all booked in advance and fully paid up. If it isn't enough for the caller he can extend with a credit card. You'll get some gay women as well. Have you got any no-go-areas?'

I asked how many readers she was recruiting. 'Any off the line?'

She hesitated and decided the answer might make me reconsider. 'A couple. Plus two guys, one gay. Don't tell Sadie.'

I didn't think Sadie would like the bearer of bad news any more than the news. I asked how she got her smoky voice.

'A tonsil op went wrong.'

What did she do before? There was always a before in this line of work. She said she'd run a club in Soho. That left plenty of room for every kind of disaster.

'How else could I be Starlight on the line? I'm the end of the line.'

I said I would have helped her if I could. She asked me again not to tell Sadie. We parted at the Engineer in Primrose Hill.

Again I sat on the top of the hill looking out across London. I understood that by working the line I had extended my consciousness, so taking in far more about people and life itself than I ever had and, if I could just let go and attune as I'd had to the tree, I would receive even more.

I started a meditation practice there and then on this hill swirling with energies and ley lines from Druid times. I became aware of my breathing and then selected a focus point, the church tower, and tried to keep the contact. I believe it was at that moment a relationship did start between my conscious thought and the atmosphere of that particular place. As I had on that afternoon with the tree I linked into the experience. It was as simple as that.

*

Three months in, and my readings were mainly with women, looking for Mr Right. The way Ray was behaving I'd be joining that queue. He had become my agent, producer, manager, but rarely lover. I had new phrases: 'Time is not easy', 'The spirit world doesn't have clocks', 'I don't want to give you false hope'. As long as I kept to the cards and kept mentioning them I felt safe. I could lay out a Celtic cross, a Circle, The Wish, 7 Card divination. I could activate my chakras, improve my breathing, read my own palm, open up to attune. It didn't make my own life any luckier. Betty was always generous with advice. 'Be interested in the caller. Tell them to ring back and let you know what's happened after the reading because you'll have some further information, and it's important they get it. In the meantime you'll link with their guides to bring luck and power.'

'Do they call back?'

'Not if they can get Grey Owl or Jade.'

*

They came on line, first the husband and then the brother.

'So, where are you getting all this from?' The husband wasn't as gentle this time and certainly didn't like the additions Lou had made to his messages. I think it was then I realised I was in to something more colourful than conversion. 'You don't answer me. Where do you know this from? I think from a place a little less spiritual than the next realm. Who told you to say this?'

The brother took the phone and said I wasn't very successful giving proof of afterlife. He was deadly, his voice artificial, cutting, and cold. If perfume had a sound this would be it. It seemed the message from Lou translated as directions the brother should take. Nothing spiritual about that one.

Should I ask for guidance from the management? Go to Sadie Chill? Maybe I was getting clairvoyant because I could hear what came next. 'Off with her head.' I had ten days to go before Worthing so I'd say nothing. I dreaded Lou's call but if she was trying to get through she couldn't reach me. I got women with the hots for their handymen, three in a row and each man putting in a new kitchen. Was it the same with another room or did this nurturing area provoke unsuitable passion? Each woman believed her handyman was in love with her, but the man felt unworthy to say so or shy or worried about his marriage, or hers. I heard about molten, hot eye contact as he installed the oven, the fact he was available at any hour, the energy between them more electric than anything he was putting in that kitchen. Personally I thought in each case the handyman would do pretty well anything to keep the money coming in and if it took molten hot looks they'd be provided. Then I got three women on the trot, all called Frances. I had to admit there were patterns out there in the ether. I thought it was the guides' way of playing a joke. The only problem – I had no idea of the guides.

And then I got Lou. 'Have you got something to tell me, Isis?' There was an edge but it was playful. Hopefully.

'Of course.' I went straight into the call from the husband and his response, forgetting completely the work deal with the line, a caller's privacy. Then I told her that you don't tell anyone what the caller tells you.

'I know all that.' Lou allowed a moment of exasperation and then recovered herself. 'I think you're going to have to try a little harder to get him converted. And next time when I call tell me you spoke to him. Remember I pay you.'

'But you haven't called and . . .'

'Come on, Isis, some days ago you got the call, the first one,

45

and when I called you didn't mention it. And now you've had another.' Tough now, needing to soften. 'But you're an angel. I could listen to you all my life. Why don't you shuffle the cards?' She was trying to please me.

I laid out a Celtic cross and told her about the high money still showing in the cards and a legal aspect needing prudence. It was much easier reading off the tarot. I'd learned to interpret the individual cards and how they changed when in conjunction with others. They started to have meaning, each card a part of an alphabet, the different arrangements, a language.

'So we're back to the man with the sheep's wig. A judge?'

And then she asked about her husband. 'Is he still hiding in the sheep croft? Maybe he's got a thing about sheep too?' Her laughter was natural and not without delight.

I saw a man in the cards, a king of swords. The surrounding influences made him a man who got what he wanted. She liked that.

'What else?'

The funny thing was in the next spread I didn't see him at all. I didn't see a husband anywhere but didn't tell her. I did health, home, travel, those in spirit.

'I am impressed, Isis.'

I mentioned family and at her age I could risk grandparents.

'Leave out the grandparents,' said Ray, forgotten in the other room.

She heard it and breathed in sharply. 'Your spirits certainly make themselves known, Isis.' And she hung up.

Why hadn't I told her about the husband's call? I thought it was because I'd not convinced him, she'd not get the result she'd wanted and she'd drop me.

Again I told Ray to stay out when I was working. I made it more meaningful this time, but he was drawn to the drama as I was.

I did wonder about Lou. Who was she and what did she look like? I was sure cosmetic with black hair, wonderfully cut. She was slim and perfect like a mathematical symbol. I didn't think she was always in the UK but linked with Italy. She wore wonderful shoes from Milan and looked after herself whatever the cost to others. She was beautiful, it went without saying, and never ever vulnerable.

It was her encouragement that had kept me on line. Her calls certainly raised my profile with the company. I was pleased until I asked why she was doing this. Was I that good a reader? The next two callers hung up in less than five minutes. I got that answer.

CHAPTER 8

'HELLO, MY NAME'S ISIS. Welcome to the line. What's your name?'
    'I want you to select three cards. I am spreading them out slowly. Tell me when to stop.'
    Rosanne didn't waste time. 'Stop.'
    'You've got the King of Hearts.'
    'That figures.' She laughed. 'And I'm not the queen.'
    I felt some drinking had been done. 'I've got an Ace of Hearts and a temperance card which means balance and patience.'
    'Tell me about it.' She sighed.
    'Waiting. It's all about waiting for the right man. He's there.'
    'So what does he look like?' she asked.
    Yes, what does he look like? Maybe Isis knew. I sure didn't. Whatever I did I must not fall asleep. I'd been waiting for a call since midnight. Rosanne, if that was her name, sounded substantial. I knew she was voluptuous, beautiful with large well shaped lips. She had a slim waist and looked good in gypsy skirts. Men went for her. Even her birth date was on her side. She'd do even better the older she got. I told her some of it.
    'But what's the guy like? I know what I look like.'
    I asked for his date of birth. That was a gamble but turned

out right because the waiting was for a man already in her life. She'd mentioned the queen and how she wasn't it, so odds on he was married. I liked Rosanne. She was warm and open and a free spirit. I hadn't got a clue what he looked like so went for qualities and his present status. If she was on the phone about him he wasn't in the room with her.

'He's gone quiet,' I said.

'Why?'

I hadn't won that round. She wasn't convinced. 'He doesn't want to lose you,' I said, quickly. I felt that was a safe generalisation. Another one coming up. 'And he has to make a decision. He's selfish.' I thought I could risk that. I said I felt she could do better.

She laughed. 'Do you know him? It's unbelievable how right those cards are.'

I wished I could have agreed about that.

'When is he going to come back?' She called me Iris. 'Because I seriously think of ending it. Without him all bets are off.' She was cut off.

Did she mean end it with him or end it?

I dreaded Lou's next call and was not sure why. Of course I'd failed to convince the husband yet I saw no husband in the cards. Yet I was not clairvoyant. Then I knew why. Lou was the one person who believed I had a psychic ability.

A friend had dropped by for tea when the line called me out of shift hours. This friend was perhaps the last person I'd want to know of my career change. Riff said there was an urgent credit card call and I didn't have to take it as I was not logged on. His tone suggested I should take it. My ratings on line were not good enough to turn anything down. I told my friend this was a personal call, wouldn't take long, and she waited in the bedroom but I was sure she tried to hear who was calling and not miss one word. My drop out of performance was something she could not understand and was the real reason for the visit.

'Where's my husband? In the sheep croft with you?'

I was aware of the friend in the next room and made a careful reply.

'Shy?' said Lou. 'You might like him.'

So it was the threesome I suspected earlier.

She asked again about the husband and I mentioned the King of Spades.

'Is he a good lover, this King? I so hope so for both our sakes. Or will we be bored?'

Another careful reply took care of the eavesdropping manager on line and the friend in the bedroom.

'OK, OK.' Exasperated now, 'I'll call later.' And Lou was gone.

My friend couldn't wait to get out of the bedroom. 'Who was that?'

'My bank manager.' He'd be next.

'Is Ray the King of Spades?' She laughed.

'If only.'

She was watching me as though I'd surprised her. 'You don't come down the club lately.' She was in a London show with a contract till Christmas. Clubs were no problem for her. I couldn't wait to get rid of her. Then she softened, became kind. 'You're too good. That's the problem. They only want the crass, the mediocre, the mindless. It's becoming a world for idiots. They don't want quality anymore. Instant gratification is too slow for this lot.'

On her way out she said, 'You're a victim of the times.'

The next caller was matter-of-fact asking for whatever the spirit world wanted to hand him. Was this again the brother? I wasn't sure and didn't like his voice. I asked his name and date of birth and he said just keep it in the moment. Should I read the messages? Should I again get the pin disbarred treatment? I played it Sadie's way. 'I don't think I'm connecting with you. I think you'd be better with another reader.'

He didn't like it and hung up.

Lou lost no time ringing back and I said I wasn't happy passing on messages. She was certainly persuasive. She wanted a better world. Didn't I? Blocked people who wouldn't see the light destroyed all progress. 'The planet is in trouble, Isis. We've got to act. Now.'

I still wasn't persuaded.

'You've got to push my husband a bit. It's for his own good. Tell him you see his grandmother.' Sarcastic now, as she remembered Ray's interjection about grandmothers. 'You're good on those.'

I asked why she'd chosen me. Was I that good?

'But you are chosen. Your voice! Heaven-given, surely?'

She had a definite power and attraction that could be manipulative. In fact I loved her laugh and suddenly wanted to meet her. I thought she was too good to be a punter on line. Something in her voice – yes, she'd lived in the US. I hadn't noticed it before. I was getting better at voices.

'I'd love to meet you one of these days, Isis.'

My God. Was she a mind reader? Were they all mind readers? I was not and my survival was dependent on it.

'You sound so vulnerable,' she said. 'I want you to be healed. I'll send you healing.'

What was that all about exactly?

'And love. I want you to be loved.'

CHAPTER 9

IF I DIDN'T HAVE the debt mountain the psychic earnings would keep me. If I worked nine hours a day I'd pay the mortgage, some bills and a voice lesson.

Howard, the readers' support guy, had been given the job of shaping up my work.

'This reading is spiritually arranged because you need to hear something very important. Remember to say this at the beginning. Then you give the usual choice. Then go into what you see.' He paused. 'What can you see?'

Not a lot. But I had become aware of one defect. Overweight. I could hear it in the person's voice. The sound was coming from a heavy place, a little breathless. Yes, it came from within a large and ponderous structure. I could also tell the thin, brittle dieting ones. It was as though there was a fat person locked inside a thin body trying to get out. These perfection-seeking women gave themselves a hard time. I told Howard I could see colours around the caller. He wasn't impressed.

I was going to rehearse the Worthing show in a few days and wouldn't need all this mindless effort. Frankly I didn't see anything. I was good on a dead man's legs and boxes of ashes. I got by in a reading following my one intention – getting the caller to talk, releasing all that pent-up confusion and distress. If all else failed I'd become a shrink.

Howard asked if I was confident to allow a pause in my reading. Of course not. They'd hang up. I asked if other people could 'see' and he said some could. Apparently they could 'tune in' and I asked how.

'Listen to the voice and allow images to come into your mind. They come from outside. Imprints. Always recallable. Given by the guide. You can test this because the imprint will always be the same, not muddled and changeable like imagined images.'

Was it my imagination that had produced the legs, the box? What was psychic and what was my own invention?

'Can you do this, Howard?'

'I'd better had,' he said.

'What do you see for me?'

'You're getting further and further into deep shit and you can't even smell it.'

Obviously not a forecast to encourage me to come back for a reading.

*

The new caller said his name was Vinnie and I had trouble with that and spelling it out. He'd reached two minutes before we got down to business. I said I was a tarot reader.

'OK. Let's shuffle some cards.'

Vinnie came from India and had lived in the US. I felt more confident with him than any other client so far, because his cards were solid, mostly coins and earthy looking and he sounded as though what I'd say wasn't the beginning and end of anything. I told him what I saw in the Celtic spread.

'You've got that right. I am in finance. What else?'

My answers amused him. To stop anymore wasting time he said he was Number 2 in a major bank. 'Am I going to get the promotion?'

How I loathed direct questions, especially about work and from men. I tried the attunement I'd used on the tree but it took too long and he started talking.

'What's your name? Your real one. Get a cab and come down. I live in Holland Park.' And then, as an afterthought, he said, 'How old are you?'

'Ask my grandchildren.' I was about to hang up.

'Don't put the phone down. You can lay out some cards for me at my place.'

'How do you know I live in London?'

'You don't come over as provincial. And the background noises of your street.'

'Maybe you should be the clairvoyant.'

He laughed. 'Shall I send you a cab?'

It would solve problems. Number 2, global bank. I said to ask me another time. The signs weren't right tonight. This call was cut and I sat back realising how tired I'd become. He could have changed my life.

✳

Showtime in Worthing, but I didn't need to get off line as the rehearsals and PR were in London and after that I'd stay on the coast for the four week show.

Lou didn't believe the husband had not called.

'So you've told him all that and he still thinks he can stay clammed up. Do what you're told, Isis. When my husband calls you tell me.'

For once she kept the reading short. I was sure her life was on change. What else was I sure about? That I must try and take the customers for myself. That rainy day group would save my economy when I was off the air in Worthing. If I undercut Sadie's prices and offered a few minutes more I'd get the ones who'd appreciate a bargain, especially the ones who needed to talk. Perhaps they all needed to talk. Maybe that's what it was.

Nobody talked enough.

I asked Betty how I should handle my leaving. I was sure I'd kick-start my career. Almost sure.

'What? You going off abroad?'

I told her I had a commitment on the south coast.

'Ask Howard to log you on there. They just change the system. You don't want to lose your little gig on line for something on the south coast. What happens when winter comes?'

Another chilly thought. I had to believe. I'd be elsewhere in November.

'When you read for me, Betty, did you see me working the line?'

'I never remember a reading, sweetie.' She was using her on line voice and I wasn't sure I believed her. I asked one more question and said I wasn't trying it on to get a free reading.

'I know,' she said. 'You're straight. I always know the users. The answer is I see you on line and no break there. Not for the foreseeable future.'

So Worthing wouldn't do it. No career kick-start in sight.

'What are you doing on the south coast? Running a B&B?'

*

Ray shuffled the cards and turned up three spades. How I hated those. He was ready for a game, not fortune telling. He put the piles together.

'Blackjack. Get your mind off the bank.' He dealt the cards.

He won every game but I gave him no opposition. He was trying to keep me company, and said he admired me for having the guts to find some sort of solution. I took a call and made it stretch the twenty minutes. I could see more looking at my kitchen door than talking to the caller. How did you see? It was a strain just keeping them on line. The cards had to do. I told Ray I needed money for my voice teacher.

'I've just gone out of style. Haven't I?'

'Come on, pay up. You're tighter than Fort Knox. Cut and deal.'

56

'Maybe I was never in style.' I'd had two hits and done well out of it for a few years. Maybe my career span was always going to be short. Maybe fate had come into it. Since working the line I saw things differently. 'It is what it is.'

'You should have been given insurance for that loan,' he said, suddenly. 'It's their responsibility. They shouldn't have let you go up this high.'

I felt a definite vertigo thinking about my finances, but his idea made sense. I'd had my share of good looks and had a way of getting what I wanted. I'd taken the first bank manager out for an expensive lunch. He could hardly bring up the subject of my growing overdraft, sitting in luxury in that restaurant eating lobster. The next got free tickets for the Hyde Park concert. The present one just got the truth. The mountain of debt had taken nearly two years to reach above the clouds.

'Has Worthing got a pier?' he said.

'I hope so. I'm on it.'

'You can do readings there.' He gave me money for the voice lessons and went to the pub.

Vinnie always came on last thing. He'd been out on the town and this was a night cap. My readings were so bad they seemed to soothe him. Maybe they sent him to sleep.

'What do you really do?' he asked. 'You're no clairvoyant but you're astute. You survive one way or another on this line. You get away with it. I see you keep trying for better angles. Did you want to get into politics? Was that it?'

All his proud talk was OK. He got off on looking into the frailties of others. But that little speech cost him £3 and then for the fun of it he called back for another dose of advising bad psychics. He asked how much I made a night. I said I could see his grandmother. I was so tired I could see everybody's grandmother.

She caught me as I was going off line and I did consider hanging up on her. It started punitive and could get worse.

'Try harder, Isis. A little harder at conversion. My husband's swanning about, as materialistic as he ever was.'

I didn't exactly like her tone and tried for some control. 'What's it about?'

'Just get him in a nodding acquaintance with redemption.'

'He isn't your husband.' I was sure of that. He wasn't in the cards.

'Maybe and maybe not, Isis, but the poor creature hopes there's an after world. Just say the lines and keep seeing sheep.'

'He's a good man.'

'That can change.' Her laugh wasn't as light as usual. 'I don't think you're putting heart and soul into this.'

I wanted to reply I'm not your servant, but asked how could anyone deal with heart and soul while reading out a list of meaningless instructions.

'Oh, so you're becoming rebellious, Isis? Just say the words with love. Love him. Don't you think we should love everyone? Isn't that the deal? Our one chance.'

I had no idea but I didn't want to hand on any more messages. She was patient and finally got me to write some down. She rehearsed me and put flavour into the adjectives. I was sure if the husband didn't become converted he'd convert me off the line into unemployment.

'Tell him the Daily Mail might like the conversion piece. Say it's right up their street.'

It began to smell like blackmail.

'I thought about you last night, Isis.' Her voice had changed, become personal, almost arousing. 'You were there by my bed about to manifest into your physical state.'

'What did I want?' My turn to challenge her.

'Well, you would know that.'

'Where is your bed, Lou?' But she was gone.

I phoned the readers support line, wanting guidance. I said I wanted to free up from this client.

'Why?'

I realised I'd got Sadie Chill. Definitely not smart.

'Refund her money.'
'Refund. Refund. Are you mad?'
Definitely.

CHAPTER 10

AND THEN CAME THE call not even a psychic could predict. Lou wanted me to meet her husband and brother at a hotel in the West End and do a tarot reading. She described what I should wear. A red dress. That surprised me as it was what I wore performing 'Ruby Red'. I decided it didn't mean anything, at most coincidence but then she mentioned just casually 'the hill'. 'As you cross the hill.' Did she mean Primrose Hill? Was she psychic? And then it occurred to me she had readings with other psychics and possibly checked me out clairvoyantly, who I was, where I lived. I told her absolutely there would be no straying into hotels with husbands and brothers. I kept close to the line.

'Oh my!' She laughed, really amused. 'One of those who did their homework. A goody-two-shoes.'

'What about you?'

'Oh, I was born on the right side of the tracks but couldn't wait to go to the wrong. They called me Bad-girl.' More laughter. I could listen to that laugh. Also each laughing response made £1.50. I was counting, counting all the time and I was becoming mean. I was mean playing cards with Ray and he didn't call me Fort Knox for nothing.

'So you lose the chance to treble what you make in a week

on that line. I'd hardly ask you to do it without recompense. A simple reading. That's all.' She allowed a pause.

What if the company found out? Not so bad. I was leaving. What if I should be recognised? What if I couldn't read the cards? The real problem was something else altogether, but I hadn't got it yet.

Lou gave up the idea so suddenly I was taken aback. It just disappeared like the callers off the line. 'Good luck, Isis.'

It sounded very much like bad luck, Isis. I considered asking Betty who else read for Lou that could have picked me up. The hill, the red dress. But none of them knew who I was, what I wore. Except Starlight. But I was leaving in a week.

*

Worthing was wonderful but there was no money. The box-office receipts covered my hotel and expenses so the last week I commuted from London. My fans were in their late twenties, some older, none younger. This is telling you, Isis, that you are going out of fashion definitely with only the debt mountain to show for it. The audiences were great, the air was great, the friends from London loyal, but I thought I should walk out to sea and keep walking. For just a short moment the thought was real enough.

'But it's Worthing,' said Ray. 'And they love you.' He couldn't see why I took such a gig seriously. He'd brought a phenomenal amount of friends to keep it going, to paper the house, as they used to say. I managed the month but nothing came from it, no tour, no TV. I did not tell Howard to move my pin number, in fact I didn't tell him anything. As far as I was concerned Isis had transcended the perils of this world and simply metamorphosed. I had lovely seaside moments, especially in the sun on the terrace of the fish restaurant.

It was here I did my press interviews. I'd started my career by default. I'd been, as they say, scuffling as a performer on the club and pub circuit on the outskirts, and one night went to the West End to apply for a job as singing showgirl in a night club. Amongst the customers was Vic Damone, the singer, well-known some years before. He was with a showbiz group and I just joined the table. At some point Vic Damone got up in good party mood and took the spotlight singing 'Volare', an old favourite from some years back. I got up and joined him. A tabloid hack got a photograph and turned it into a story and next I was touring Europe. I did a short stop-over in Italy but can't remember much about any of it now. I didn't see Vic Damone again. In those days I was blond and very young-looking, like a waif. They said I had the beautiful untouched face of a child. In contrast my voice was smoky and had a catch in the midrange which made it quite unique. And I did jazz. Even the black singers agreed about that. It was inconceivable after the way my career took off that I could end like this. I left that out of the press story for the south coast. I left a lot out.

I got back to London to phone calls, not on line but from the bank. 'You'll have to consider the perhaps inevitable.' The manager assumed I knew the inevitable. I'd met people who'd gone belly-up, bankrupt, and they reinvented themselves and started again. As soon as I'd finished with the bank I called the line and Riff was pleased to hear from me. 'There's been callers looking for you. Usual hours?'

'Longer.' I figured if I doubled the shifts I'd have a flight fund in place. It gave a kind of relief. The debt mountain was now unstable, subject to avalanches. My best thinking was to go to the Caribbean and open a club. I had enough track for that. In the meantime I tried all the London clubs but summer was not the best time. I could do a Jazz in the Park event but the billing they offered was not acceptable. I managed backing singer for a week and then Ray got me a studio deal to cut a CD. It wasn't what I was used to but I took it with both hands. He'd get the musicians and handle distribution. I'd write two new songs and do more work with the voice teacher and we'd be ready to go late August. He was doing it to give me hope.

I said they would force me to sell the flat.

'Well, let's not go down that track. Let's keep it as though it's going to work until it doesn't.'

'It will be sudden. I'll just drop out.' Perhaps I'd become Isis and that made me laugh. 'Come on, Ray. No one will touch me. I can't even give myself away.'

No more calls from Lou. She'd obviously got a more acquiescent reader. I asked Betty for the latest news and she was involved in a bitter dispute with Jade, the top reader.

'She is in direct opposition to my make-them-feel-good approach. She's studying to be a psychotherapist and believes in truth. She sees it helping others to face reality. Who wants reality? I could see the point.

I started to slip away back to Worthing to the hotel with the lovely view right on the sea and a calm that promised only good things.

The row between Jade and Betty over reading policy divided the company and the Queen of Hearts had to step in, prepared to cut off heads. No reader must ever criticise, condemn or try and change another. She insisted no reader was superior. That gave me a laugh. Jade and Grey Owl. What were they if not superior? They were certainly fattened up for that role by getting the cream of the bookings. And the guides might want one outcome or another, but that was irrelevant when it came to the company. For all the psychic chatter the company wanted results and that was long duration calls, repeat callers and pure profit. My policy was to keep the reader for the full twenty minutes. I was now offering love, career and home and saw more or less the same for each caller. I gave an identikit picture of Mr Right and it was amazing how many Mr Rights it fitted.

'But he's just like the one I've met. How can you know?'

I was as mystified as they were.

Sadie Chill said, 'Now, darling, if a reader asks you directly if his wife or her husband is being untruthful do not say yes. You can't be sure and saying yes can break up a marriage.'

This was a lot of words from her about a simple aspect of the readings. I guessed someone had, under pressure from a caller, given in and agreed it was yes. Yes, the bastard is screwing his PA in all ways in all locations.

'Go for the other aspects of the relationship. Deal with the fear. Get them thinking less obsessively. Let them remember the love. They still can love. And their own personal freedom.' Then she added, 'Relationships end like everything else but there's always a choice as to how. Let it be loving. And make your readers listen to you. You need minimum twenty minutes.'

'What if they can't afford it?'

She paused in honour of the very idea. It was unthinkable. 'They need to hear it so they'll find a way to afford it. That's why they're on line.'

I went back to her earlier statement. 'What do you mean relationships end like everything else?' I was worried suddenly about Ray.

'The planet is impermanence.' The purpose of her call for all those words seemed slight and as I thought there had been something behind it. A husband whose wife had left him after a reader had said he was unfaithful wanted Sadie Chill's blood. He'd gone to the press. Betty said the reader was an old-timer and wouldn't make mistakes. He was now an ex-old-timer.

✳

When I came back from walking on Primrose Hill there was a message waiting from Betty. 'A new excitement in town.' A guru had come over from India and no one had ever seen anything like her. Sadie had proclaimed her a divinity. I phoned Betty, thinking we were going to get this person on line.

'Oh, no, she gets us on her line. We're going to make up a party to see her. There's a supper afterwards.'

'She's a direct incarnation of one of those with impossible names. Apparently she changes everything just by the sound of her voice.'

Starlight was the only reader who knew my identity as it faded into the past. She wouldn't tell, not all the time I knew she ran a rival line, but I still I told Betty I could not go.

'Sadie says we have to and it will help our readings.'

I offered myself immediately as a sacrifice so others would go. I'd stay on line and handle the calls. I suspected Betty could be the management spy because the Queen of Hearts lost no time telling me sacrifice was something the management decided upon and missing this opportunity at the Albert Hall was flying in the face of evolvement. I told her I'd seen so many Indians peddling evolvement over the years.

'But she's not Indian.'

I waited to hear what she was.

'She's lived in India in retreat since childhood. She's white, so be at the restaurant, there's a love. All paid for.'

She would recognise me. I'd have to be ill.

I saw a picture of the guru Shanti Opal in the evening paper. She was beautiful, deeply beautiful, out of touch of us mere mortals yet ready to approach with tenderness and compassion. Long sun bright hair flamed around her, her body well covered up, was certainly voluptuous. She'd been born on an island in the Pacific and remembered from earliest age her previous incarnation as a divinity, and aged four, was taken back to the residence she'd described on the Ganges. In this life she'd studied with the spiritual masters for some years but already had located enough insight from previous existences to teach them. She gave Darshan at nine years of age, her life purpose to share, to instruct. Like modern-day gurus she'd been told to leave isolation and take her teachings to the West. Her age wasn't given but I thought she'd reached thirty. Incongruously, I thought she looked like Marilyn Monroe.

After a gruelling afternoon in the bank during which I came

to some arrangement to start reducing the debt mountain I called in on my agent. He could offer me the Low Countries and a fee for sitting on a talent scout jury on ITV. I said I'd do both. I went home utterly depressed and decided to cancel definitely the psychics' dinner and Albert Hall performance. I realised this meant I couldn't go on line, but suffering from a mercifully short migraine I could log on at 10 p.m. and work till dawn. The sadness of my sinking career left me almost unable to speak but the heartache did something. I could understand another's pain.

Against a background of night time fusion between the earth and other realms, I spoke to the lonely looking for love, completeness, a new life, magic, their deceased partners. Some needed to talk, others to be cheered up. Apparently there were celebrities using the line, political, religious, show-biz, musical, but I got the housewives. They wanted the means to put a curse on a rival or to release themselves from the hell of arranged marriage and be with the one they really loved, usually someone else's husband, a brother-in-law or driving instructor. After a few weeks on line was there anything I didn't know? Some begged me almost crying to give them their husband's not date of birth but date of death. Most were keen on curses and expected them to be available. What had I got to offer? Only the usual sort.

Betty said the guru was out of this world. 'I can't believe I'm saying this with my life, but through her I can reach something better. I'll never forget it.'

Naturally I asked if the guru was fake. It was the obvious question. It so upset Betty she hung up.

Ray was strangely taken by the accounts of the guru evening. 'Some of them went from the orchestra and said she's quite out of this world. I think it's an act, but so what if it makes people feel that good.' He paused. 'Maybe we should go and see her.'

Shanti Opal had rave commentary in the tabloids and she was obviously some kind of phenomenon. I'd seen the Maharishi and tried TM. I'd seen the Bagwan and managed to keep hold of my money which in his presence was rare. I'd been to Mother Meera and had the experience of her gazing into my eyes. I'd heard teachings of Sy Baba. I'd been to Lourdes. I'd rather be on line.

Starlight had secretly recorded Shanti Opal and had got some of it clearly on tape in spite of background noise cutting in. As I listened to these short passages that were audible I could identify the sound of someone used to getting their way. Her voice seemed to take over and I was as chemically changed as if I'd been given an anaesthetic. There was no doubt about it. Of course she used a technique to raise the crowd to hysteria. Of course it would be hypnotism. Starlight was less impressed than Betty but had to agree a change had been effected in her and she'd go again. Using rhythmic chants the guru lifted the mood of the crowd and introduced a compelling message of hope. She herself sounded under some influence yet her accent was unexceptional and hard to place. It seemed to hold the resonances of all the localities she had visited. Hers was a mongrel accent. There was certainly an American touch. Starlight talked while her tape ran silently to the end and there we discovered another short message overlooked. The guru said, 'I love you, Isis.'

I asked her to replay that section and whatever she did she must not make some terrible mistake and erase anything. I wasn't sure of her common sense in ordinary life. Hearing it again only confirmed the fact. This was Lou's message.

'Do you remember her saying that?'

'What?'

'I love you, Isis.'

'But it's not that. She said, "I love you. Ice is no defence." She replayed that section. "Before my love even ice will melt and . . ." The tape was running out, and I think she said, "You will have no chance . . ."'

I wanted to know how and when she'd made that statement.

'Towards the end. She talked of the language of the heart.

She has a voice you just want to go on hearing.'
I asked if I could have a copy of the tape. I knew she wouldn't
know how to do it herself and suggested getting it from her and
burning off some copies. I also knew arranging a time would
be difficult.

'I love you, Isis.' Was I now hallucinating? Had I been on
line so much my reality was frazzled, letting in all sorts of bits
of memory. I'd better cut down the shifts. I had to wait to get
hold of Betty and see what she remembered. Now she thought
about it there was something odd and contrived about that
small sentence.

'She did bring in ice but she could just have easily said
something else. Ice was clumsy considering the rest of it. And
she jumbled it together. "Ice is."'

Hallucinations – no, paranoia – possibly. Suspicious –
definitely. I told Ray we must go the very next night, but he was
playing so I rang to book a seat. Standing room only and this
was the last performance.

The following evening I waited at the edge of a mass of
people already told getting in was unlikely. There was talk of
a screen being put up and the performance could be watched
outside. I think it was here at this moment I knew I had dropped
from sight. I wasn't just low. I was invisible. What was I doing
standing on the outside of a performance hall? I should be
inside on stage. I remembered one of the sound technicians and
tried to see if he was on duty. I couldn't even get in the staff
door. I even said my name. Had things come to this? The chaos
was extreme, then fizzled out as the crowd gave up and left. The
show had started.

Ray's friend in the violins took me for a drink and said
Shanti Opal was not a new phenomenon. She'd been going for
years in the Middle East, Australia and the US. He believed she
was around thirty and unmarried. She had a good message and
a superb delivery. Did he believe it? He paused enough to take
it seriously.

'I think she's the result of big business. They run her and make thousands out of it. Performances, ashrams, donations. And she self-hypnotises. It has to be that. But she is a star. But maybe the tidal wave is over. Are gurus still business?'

I asked where she went next but he thought she had no more bookings.

'She's done the States. She'll probably start again in September in the Far East. That's what she usually does.'

'Who runs her?'

He didn't know.

So I asked about the amazing sentence, and he had another explanation altogether. 'She did run it all at once. That's right. She was going to end there, "I love you", but as an afterthought went back to the earlier mention of ice. The ice age before known time. The Fall. The planetary changes, gravity . . .'

'Could she have said "I love you, Isis"?'

'Yes, she could.'

'Is she fake?'

'I don't know. She's got an intelligent and well-heeled following. I don't think they'd go for fake.'

✳

I apologised to Sadie Chill and used the occasion to ask about the guru.

'She does what she's here to do. Raise the level of consciousness and connect to the heart chakra in all of us.'

'Does she use hypnosis?'

'Of course. She sends out a musical note F sharp which brings awareness up to exultation. Everyone is bound into one sound, one essence. Of course it can become an out-of-body experience.'

'But it's a technique.'

'In us it is a technique. For her, something else. She is a divinity reborn. What about your reading durations? They have to be increased.'

I would have asked about the Isis moment, but the rush of criticism had started. I said I would try to work from the edge without falling off it. That made her laugh.

CHAPTER II

THE WOMAN WAS ROUGH and ready for trouble. She was older than the date of birth she gave me, and if her name was Martina I'd eat the tarot pack. I also felt there were other people present and I was sure I'd heard the sound of suppressed laughter. There was certainly a splashing sound as something heavy was placed in water. Was she taking a bath? I gave her the usual choice and started on the one she wanted. Wealth. She stopped me halfway.

'You know it's crap what you're saying. You say the same thing to everyone. This costs me £1.50 a minute.'

'Then why spend your money?' I said.

'I have to work for mine,' she answered.

'Then don't waste it on this.'

'No, keep reading. I like you. I like the fact you're not in it only for the money.'

I must have got something right because she kept on talking even when I wanted to give her information.

'Don't worry padding it out, darling. We're all in the same business as you – my friend Julie here and Boo and young Max. But we reckon you're all right.'

'So you're psychics?'

That got a laugh. 'No, we're on the sex line. We only get 18 pence a minute to your 33, so we're the poor cousins. My name's Sharon, by the way.'

I asked what the sex line was like.

'You just read from a script and put the voice on. But the script doesn't always have the answer to some of their requests.'

That got a laugh.

'The psychics think they're better than us. Especially that snotty Jade.'

I asked if they worked for Starlight.

'She's been around for years. You want to watch out with her. She tries to grab everything.' She stopped. 'So what do I look like?'

I told her I had no idea.

'At least you're honest. We're supposed to be twenty, dressed in sex knickers and bras with huge boobs, hungry for it. I'm sixty-six and my feet hurt. I've been on them all day. I'm sitting here putting them in a bucket of water and Epsom salts. My hair's in pins and my teeth out. I've got a woolly dressing-gown that looks like an old rug. I weigh sixteen stone and can't lose one ounce. My face may be shiny with cream but you see, love, I know how to talk to the punter and I can pretend to be sixteen. Eileen here is chopping onions and making a decent cook-up for later. You ought to try it with us. At least you'd get a laugh.'

I agreed about that.

'Watch out for deception. Comes from a woman. Yes, darling, I'm an old gypsy. Romany family. Three Jacks and a Black King. Not a good thing.'

I wondered why they'd spent the money. Testing the talent on the rival line cost them £30. I found out they were testing me for the sex line. This was another job I didn't get offered.

I knew Mrs Longbridge would be back. This time, she had a speedier delivery but certain vocal sounds you could not conceal. Usually it was the vowels or the speech rhythm. Sometimes Mrs Longbridge's short A was flat. And that slight

Welsh touch when emotions heated up. Tonight she was known as Rose and wanted to know what I could see. The armchair, the man unmoving, rotting by now and the box and the sunlight streaming in and money all over the floor. I couldn't tell her any of this. I had no idea what she'd do about it. How dangerous she could be if I knew after all what should not be known. She rang back immediately and I did wonder if she could afford it. She was ringing because if I couldn't see what was in that room she was safe. I did pass this one through Betty.

'Oh, we've all had her.'

I asked what they'd got.

'She just wants to be one ahead. Lonely and bitter and no one to put it on. Used to put it on the husband.'

'Where is he?'

'Gone.'

'How?'

'One way or another.'

I asked how much Mrs Longbridge spent on line and Betty thought £60 a night. I asked if she could afford it.

'Let her worry about that. You need her to keep on thinking she can afford it.'

Another three hang-ups in a row and then I got Vinnie whose latest entertainment was to pretend to be other people. He gave different names and birthdates and once or twice had me fall for it, but like Mrs Longbridge, there was one sound, a certain rhythm or resonance he wasn't aware of and so didn't do anything about it. I let him play the game and pretended I was reading for Charles Frost, the upper-class Englishman on line for the first time and stuffed in a lot I knew about Vinnie. If he was surprised by my skill he didn't show it. At other times halfway through I'd say to Willy Lomax from Kansas, 'Hey you're Vinnie. My God, you're good.' Sex line next, Babe. Try and keep some standards.

Some sound in a person's voice was unique as a finger print and there was no way they could turn it off. I wondered about

Lou and her voice patterns and asked Starlight again for a copy of the tape. I even asked the Albert Hall if she had a management company looking after her. Ray looked her up on the Net and she worked out of an ashram in India, which handled all mail and enquiries. I did try and call them and got a recorded message in several languages giving the dates and places of Shanti Opal's appearances which were, I noticed, all in the past. It would not have occurred to me that the voice I'd heard on the tape was Lou's except for that one probably misinterpreted message. Or Lou had got to the guru and asked for the inclusion. Maybe she was the 'they' with the money.

Lily with a credit card booking for an hour paid my gas bill. I began to see the point of Betty's approach as opposed to Jade's. Keep on their side. Make them feel good. I tried to find a moment of connection and then encourage a state of lovingness. I'd never tell Ray or anybody but it was the start of being able to reach another human being. I found I was on their side.

CHAPTER 12

IT TOOK A FEW seconds to realise it was Lou on the line and then I was pleased, even relieved. She was back. I said I was pleased to hear from her.

'Make the most of it, Isis, because you won't be.'

'I take it your husband isn't going for the messages.' I remembered, how could I not? that she'd told me to wear a red dress and she'd mentioned the hill. Her voice didn't sound anything like the Albert Hall slightly hypnotic voice I barely remembered from the tape.

'You're not getting through to him, Isis. And that's impossible. So I wonder why?'

I questioned the 'impossible'. She ignored that and said I was most probably contrary and a part of me wanted the opposite result. Was she a shrink? Was that it?'

'You seem to know a lot about me yet you've never met me.'

'Oh, I know you.' Her voice was back to the light, loving one of earlier calls. 'We've known each other before.'

'When?'

'Perhaps in other lives? I'd know you amongst a thousand people in Manhattan at noon. Alone in a jungle in Columbia. Bathing in the Ganges.' I decided she was teasing me. 'So what

I suggest is you meet my husband as I asked you to and read his cards. Allow the spirit to come through. I'll prepare your little speech. Just learn it. You get well paid.'

'What if he asks questions?'

'Oh, I think you can handle that.'

I did pause. I was so sick of being trapped on line. 'Where will this take place?'

She thought a hotel off Park Lane.

'Will you be there?'

'Not obviously.'

I did think about it for all of two seconds. As dramatic as I could be about small things, I didn't believe Sadie Chill had set this up to test me. I wasn't a good enough reader. I didn't go for it because I wasn't sure I could carry it off and what if I was still remembered and they recognised me. It was over a year since my last TV appearance. But I didn't turn her down completely. I asked for time.

'You've got it. For now. He's not in town. You'll be called when it's set up.'

I didn't answer.

'Don't you want to know how much your fee might be?'

I said I was sure it would be correct.

'You've not still got that snooty attitude about money. Things must have reached a pretty state of affairs for you to be on this line.' Her voice changed with her mood. 'So get sharp, Isis.' She was hard and it wasn't what she wanted me to see. 'Remember to wear a red dress. And think of the fee. Think of it as you walk over the hill. I mean metaphorically. Is that too sharp for you?'

'Why red?'

'I can see red suits you.'

'Maybe you should be the psychic.'

'Everybody has some psychic ability. They just have to develop it.'

'And the hill?'

She didn't hesitate. 'I feel you're having to climb a hill right now. Will that do?' She seemed to sigh.

'Do you talk to other psychics?'

'Not since finding you, Isis.'

'But you ask them about me.'

'Not a chance. You're easy to read. Where do you want your fee delivered?'

I said I had to think about it. 'It's not remotely in this job description.'

She paused. 'Just get your head out of the sheep trough and work on my husband.'

She hung up.

*

Increasingly I thought about a club which I'd start on my own and get some good performers and A-list audience. Where did I get the backing? I wondered how much Lou's fee would have been. Could I have gone on reading for the husband and then the brother? I'd been four months on line and had a few regular customers. My delivery was now slick and quick, but with some callers like Rosanne I felt I must take away the pain. The flight fund had enough for the Bahamas one way and I put a third of the line money into that, another third paid the voice teacher and the bank got the rest. I never thought this would happen to me.

'I never thought this would happen to me.' Her name was Virginia and her life had crashed. What could I see? Not a lot. Who did she remind me of? Virginia hadn't been on line before. She had a smart voice and had had an enviable performing career. She let me know that but as I wasn't psychic I couldn't see in what area. I told her what I'd just told myself and meant every word of it. It was the daily spiritual upper sometimes taken hourly.

'But do you see me going on with my – it's not work. It's a vocation, Isis.'

I really hoped I did. Luckily we were cut off. Who did she

remind me of? Myself.

Sadie Chill on the message system: 'Stop asking them questions, Isis. You're supposed to see both the answer and the question.' I was trying my best but my days were numbered. I didn't have to be psychic to see that.

Ray said he'd take on more concert work and rent out his flat. We'd do the CD and plan the UK tour. He liked the club idea and said he'd look around. He was too nice and then it occurred to me I'd heard this a few times from the callers. Didn't they, the men, always become too nice when they were anything but? A hundred women would sign their name on that line. Did he have someone else? Was he about to drop me? We had a serious talk about money which made me suddenly doubtful about everything. Was it my last gig at the Hyde Park concert over a year ago that was to blame? I didn't quite hit it and I hadn't got them on my side. Suddenly I thought of other two hit singers who suddenly dropped out. Or life dropped them. It happened. Ray said I had emotional power, especially in the old French songs, and a thrilling sound. I was a cult performer. He said he could see me sitting on a stool at a bar in a club in Paris doing Autumn Leaves. Hair up in a French style, my voice smoky, singing for the love of it. I'd hit them then. He was more polite than I'd known him. Was it a woman? Didn't I hear this on line every second night? 'He started to be careful, then sweet, then gone. I should have known.' Maybe I should move myself to Paris and save myself from this new lot of pain.

'It was the Hyde Park gig, wasn't it, that broke me? Bob saw it right as it happened.'

'No. Ruby Red was too big and gave a false sense of the future. Maybe I'm being psychic. Being in here is catching. But you couldn't pull it with the songs you did later. It had nothing to do with Geldorf or the others. Sheree came along. She was fifteen years younger than you and took the town. She was wild, you were nostalgic. She ended up with your gigs.'

The phone rang and I didn't take it.

'Are you going to put in new material?' He was talking about the CD.

I said I would. I'd have to feel more optimistic, more energetic, more courageous. I was out of style and getting old for the territory. The phone rang again and Arnold, who'd replaced the latest cut off your head victim Riff, told me to get on line. I was late, and customers were waiting.

Maybe I should change careers. At least in this one I was wanted.

✳

Rosanne's voice was unrecognisable. It was drenched with tears, raw with grief. Paul didn't want her. He didn't ever want to see her again.

'I'll phone the wife. I'll tell her. I'll go to the door.'

I tried to talk her out of that one. 'Can you afford the readings?'

She said she could. She didn't want me to say anything, just listen. If he was definitely gone she'd be gone too. I asked what she meant.

'I'll top myself.'

'Rosanne, that is not in the scheme of things. Not remotely. It won't solve anything. It's wrong. The spirit world abhors suicide.' How did I know this? 'Stay here and sort it out. It will be much better here than over there.' Yes, I did believe suddenly in 'over there'.

'Can you afford this, Rosanne? Yes or no?' I meant, calling the line.

'No,' she said, quietly.

'Then take my mobile number. Call me only when it's absolutely necessary.'

I gave it to her and she thanked me and was gone. I felt filled with an energy as though the north wind was rushing through me. I was filled with the fight to keep what should be here, here. It was the first time I felt my reading became work and could be valuable.

Several days later, and nothing from my agent, I decided

to phone venues myself. I couldn't let go, couldn't believe this crash had happened. Worthing hadn't paid off – nothing came from it. The good London venues were booked until early next year. Why couldn't I let go?

Every caller was Lou until they turned into Karen or Sharon, or incomprehensible names from the East. Ninety per sent were nice, friendly and wanted the best result. The others, trouble.

'Iris, please tell me if it is the end with Paul?'

I wondered if there had ever been a beginning. His wife was now pregnant for the fourth time. So I learned a new trick. Bring in the next man. Keep him vague but give him form. 'He's got a dry humour and his one-liners crack you up. He's physical and not afraid to love women. He makes you feel complete.'

It was amazing how many wanted just that. Come to think of it, didn't I?

'You should do Valentine cards,' said Ray.

So I turned on him and asked if he didn't have more to do than watch my boat going down. That mark on his neck! A love bite? Was I becoming over-sensitised to my thoughts? Paranoia next. Did other readers go through this?

Lou was next and I could almost smell her perfume. She didn't waste time. The address was off Park Lane, the time 8 p.m. tonight. A car could pick me up or I could make my own way and charge the fare. I'd be met in the entrance and taken up to the hotel suite.

'How will he recognise me?' Smart now.

'Because you'll wear a red dress. Here's how it goes: get a pen and write the following.'

It was a short message which I must learn and it seemed to promise no peace until the man recognised the light worker who'd done so much for him and honoured his obligation. She changed 'honoured' to 'fulfilled' and back again. I was to surround the message with my usual psychic fill-up. After thirty minutes I would put the cards together, stand up, nod briefly, and leave.

'Wear your adornments. Put it all on. You know how to do it.

D'you want the fee in fifties?'

'I am not a messenger.' I realised suddenly that I was.

She laughed. 'It pays well.' She said a price I would not have believed.

I was about to ask her if she had got to the guru at the Albert Hall to give me a message, but felt unsure. I was now on unsure ground. Why had she chosen me? I wasn't that good.

'Do a good job tonight. There's more where that comes from.'

*

I started the daily voice exercises but didn't finish. I didn't sing anymore. I sat like a broken bird on the stiff chair, down-hearted. Singing had been my life. I realised I was in bereavement for what had been.

At six o'clock on this summer evening I did start getting ready for the meeting in Park Lane and I even got the red dress, the one I used for 'Ruby Red.' Sadie Chill's earlier warnings about meeting the clients privately arrived clearly in my mind. She'd said the company would not give a moment of protection for a reader's betrayal. And how dangerous it could be. She'd backed it up with horror stories. I thought mine might join that list. So I took the dress off and chose the songs I'd record for the CD. It would start and end with 'Ruby Red' which was said to be based on a ritual chant from ancient Egypt.

I expected Lou would ring but the first call was Mrs Longbridge, then Rosanne, then Vinnie. The heat of the night was terrible and I had to open all the windows and let the street noise in. I answered the fourth call but couldn't hear her properly and she repeated her opening accusation.

'So you chickened out.'

She did sound American. I closed a window.

'It's not part of my job description.'

She sighed. 'I don't know quite what I'll do about this.'

'Not a lot, Lou. You don't know me.'

'I've always known you. From the moment I heard your voice.'

'I'm not a messenger.'

'Oh, but you are.'

I didn't like that. 'Why do you want me? There are better readers.'

She didn't answer.

'I'm so good? Is that why you chose me?'

'No. Because you're so bad.'

For some inexplicable reason I was shocked. The 'so bad' actually surprised me. Had I really thought it could be otherwise? And then I got the 3 a.m. call.

'Baa, Baa, Black Sheep, three bags full. They'd better be.' Hang up.

It took a moment to realise I had been asleep, in bed, logged off the line. How had she got my private number? I dialled 1471 to trace the call but the number was withheld. I got up, made tea, leaned out of the window and the heat was hardly less than it was in the afternoon. They said it would hit 100 degrees and some people were thrilled. I covered my head with a wet towel and then I realised Ray wasn't in. How many times had I heard this story on line. Certain items in the fridge had gone off, and the fridge was clattering, doing its best. Like me, I thought, and laughed. Of course I was in something other than clairvoyance. 'Baa Baa Baa' was not about three red kings or luck, money, change. She'd even sounded like a sheep.

CHAPTER 13

THE MAN PHONED FIVE times and wanted to know about his wife. It was only on the fourth that I understood she was dead. I tried to talk about the process of leaving the body and going into the next realm. To me it sounded like being born into this one. I'd heard it described during the sessions in the Psychic Research College when I tried to locate my guide. The man phoned a fifth time to see if I could get anything more. I recommended he try Jade. He said his small son was inconsolable. It was one of the hardest calls I'd had and I could tell him only that it would change, this anguish into acceptance and that he would have an understanding of her progress in spirit and know that she was more than all right. Where I got that from I couldn't guess, but it seemed to speak through me rather than from me. It wasn't the result of my striving to find consoling words. He didn't want consolation or sympathy. He needed me to be strong and find death normal. I did say something about a small sheep, I was good on sheep and he said that was the last toy she'd given their son. At the end of the call I wanted to weep but I got Carl, the young financier, who wanted in at a global corporation in the City. He'd been for the recall interview. Would he get the job? I had to box around with that one. I said it would be his choice

and he had to watch the small words in the contract.
'It's called "watch the small print". Anyone could say that.'
He still sounded nice enough.

'So, Isis, what d'you get on the new company?'
He had a nasal voice and I wished he'd ask about his health.
I could deal better with the sinus problems resulting probably
from coke. Amazingly he stayed on line. Perhaps because he was
on coke, or after four months I had some sort of confidence.
I got the subject out of the City and into the bedroom. I was
better with that side of life.

No Mrs Longbridge these days. I supposed she'd found
a better victim. And then Betty told me the woman had been
stopped credit and was facing bankruptcy. She'd spent thousands
on line.

'It's bad for the company because it makes us look as though
we're feeding her addiction.'

'Aren't we?'

'How can we when she uses different names, dates of birth
and voices?'

'Subject matter?'

'Betty thought about that. 'She always wanted to know
what I could see. I called it the living-room and she said why do
people call it a living-room? Why not a dying-room?'

It will hit the tabloids and Sadie won't like that. She's a right
one, Sadie, and wouldn't let a customer get in trouble. If she
sees they're on too much she talks to them and suggests other,
often free, alternatives.'

I asked if a client could get a reader's personal number. She
said it was impossible. The technical staff would cop it, truly.
Off with their heads? Off with everyone's head.

'What about past workers?' Now I was thinking of Riff. 'If
someone paid enough.'

'If they've that kind of dough what would they be doing with
someone like Riff? They wouldn't even be able to find a Riff.'

I did ask Grey Owl and Arnold and was assured it had never

happened. When Lou next called I would ask direct questions but Lou didn't call and I was surprised that days past without another off hours taunt. Then it occurred to me if she had my private number she might have my address. For a while, a short while I did look around me as I left the flat but I had other things to think about.

We put the CD together in heat beyond belief. My feet were in buckets of what once was cold water reminding me of the women on the sex line. My head was covered with bags of dripping ice cubes. Every fan in the place was full blast. The studio manager suggested we move into a hotel with air-conditioning and work there. Performers with money had started living at The Landmark off the Marylebone Road. I was no longer one of those, and Ray was quick to suggest we just go for it in one day, all bets off. I was hardly a beginner but it took until dawn. The tech boys would sleep a few hours, do the cut and give me first approval. It was the cheapest recording I'd ever done and Ray kept saying this was the way things would go. It'll all be net produced and net sold. I hoped he had a little more in mind for my distribution. The plan was to get it out there before my UK tour began late summer.

In the first light of dawn we walked barefoot across Primrose Hill and my mobile rang and Rosanne said she was desperate and could I give her a few moments. She didn't know how to get through the next seconds.

'Can't they leave you alone? Even at the end of the night.' Ray was irritated and I knew he found the change in me difficult. Maybe Rosanne's problem was closer than I thought. Was he with someone else? I told him about the out-of-hours call from Lou. 'You must have slipped her your number when you were tired. Well, you gave it to this other one. Maybe she got it from her?'

I hadn't thought of that.

I got a cluster of guys in finance. Some of them had big positions in big banks and the very thought they could be looking to a clairvoyant for guidance terrified me.

'Isis, just answer me this. Does the boss trust me? More. Should I trust him?'

I said trust was not a commodity for him to deal in. Survival was more appropriate.

'Isis, the number 3 in Citi keeps putting off our meeting. Is he thinking of trading with someone else?'

'He was always thinking of trading with everyone else. He thinks laterally.'

'So should I trust him?'

'Not until he gives you reason to trust him.'

'Now just look at the markets and tell me if the dollar is gonna go weak against the euro.'

I stretched my mind until I thought it would crack, trying for some glimmer of what the future held. I gave answers these guys seemed to believe. And these guys run the money markets. I'd be running the world next. It was a catastrophic thought.

'Cool down,' said Ray. 'You talk to five guys. There are 50,000 of them out there.'

I was on every night from the first slot staying sometimes till dawn. I could do nearly a hundred pounds, sometimes more a day and I put the extra hard-earned money into the flight fund. I was more like Betty than Jade but didn't agree with everything the callers said or promised them they'd get what they asked for. I found a point in each caller where I could draw close. I was on their side and I began to have care for them and that became the real purpose of the exchange. Just love them unconditionally, no matter what they'd done. Maybe I was the only person all week who gave them any contact. Often I was so exhausted by dawn my eyelids stuck and my messages became part of sleep's early dreams. And then I slid into sleep and woke up with the phone dangling by my ear. If the caller was still there I'd say I'd been in a trance and located their guides. In the end I could get myself out of anything.

Backed up by Ray, I confronted the bank about the insurance they must have insisted I take on a loan so large. It seemed I wasn't advised to take any and Ray decided that was negligent. The bank must be responsible for the debt mountain. How did I know my career would crash? I'd made enough in the lucky years to assume everything would continue. Although I was a two-hit singer my career was bigger than that and had lasted. How did I know when it simply stalled it had died? I'd just gone on expecting work, looking for work. I got rid of the car, the cottage in the country, and slowly the habits. Ray said he'd get me legal advice.

The UK tour would start in the autumn and slowly my agent managed to book a few venues, the sort that showed I'd known better times. The CD was out there and getting some support from radio stations. The agent was still trying for television and was sure I'd at least get local coverage in the areas I toured. I wasn't sure about anything. More and more I felt like my clients on line. How did I know it would be all right? How did I know I'd even be on line? Sadie Chill had axed three readers and was recruiting new talent. I knew to stay away from Sadie, not give her anything to react to, even the strange matter of Lou's next out of hours sheep call. 'Baa, Baa, Baa, Better be'. It was after 5 a.m. and I was still in deep sleep. I had automatically picked up my phone and would have given the psychic's introduction: 'Bags full, Isis.' It felt as though her voice was all around the room. I hung up and took the receiver off the hook. My mobile rang and, sleep over, I got up and found the phone. It showed a withheld number and I asked how she'd got mine. I was quite friendly which surprised me. She was hard. 'I'm psychic too. Be very sharp now, Isis. Just think nice clear thoughts and you'll know what you have to do. Just keep telling yourself I must put my trust in the right people.'

'I'm no messenger.' I sighed.

'Think again. You connect spirit with the caller. Isn't that being a messenger? Better be or it only takes one call.'

Did she mean to the spirit world? She meant to the company. 'One call and you're dumped. So think of me as your custodian.

You haven't done so well on your own.'

She clicked off and I looked at the vacant screen on my phone and I did think nice clear thoughts. She knew too much and it certainly wasn't through psychic channels. Someone had told her things and on the shortlist was Starlight, Sadie Chill and Riff. What about Ray? These were 5 a.m. thoughts touched with fear. Why Ray? Favours done for information. Lou had offered me enough for a simple card reading with the commentary already provided. Ray needed money because I did. He certainly saw things differently and wouldn't think that revealing me was deceiving me if it meant he could keep me going. My standing orders and card payments alone meant we could no longer lead the life ordinary people did. When did we last go out? I started looking at Ray differently. When he said not to worry about the electric bill was it because Lou was already paying it.

The company said I could log on whenever I wanted. I was given more credit calls and my income improved. I thought this was because I'd cut it as a psychic, but Betty said the schools had broken up for summer and many readers had to drop the line to look after children or go on holiday.

The money guys were not on holiday. They wanted answers to impossible questions. One of them said: 'I know your voice. I've heard it before. Are you famous?' I said the Andy Warhol famous for fifteen minutes line. Next I recognised 'the brother', his perfumed malice would not be forgotten easily. 'They tell me you're the sharpest one on line. Give me some of the sharp.' Lou had been to work on him, written his lines. I remembered 'sharp' from the nocturnal call. 'So what's in the message box?'

'I do not give messages.'

'But you do.'

'Nothing coming through for you.'

'Too bad, Toots. You bite the hand that feeds you.' Hang up. She'd put him up to it.

I didn't wait long for her call. She sang a line, just one of

'Ruby Red' and hung up.

The next day I understood the full implication of my association with Lou. By fate or ill luck I was pulled into a world of probable crime. The brother's voice belonged in bad places. I was not a good but a bad clairvoyant, and that's what they'd needed. My job was to work on the husband and amaze him or frighten him into giving them what he thought he could withhold. Serious money was involved. For some reason I was indispensable perhaps because I knew too much, or they'd sold him the idea of me. Maybe he was a fan. A diminishing species. I felt scared to go out, to answer the phone, to go near the windows. Should I run for it? Did I have enough in the flight fund? They knew who I was and where I lived. And then the mobile started and Rosanne desperately needed help. Rosanne and her problem lover now got on my nerves, and I was sharp with her and said only call when she was really in trouble. The private phone rang, then the mobile, there was a bell ringing upstairs and then a knocking at my door. I'd definitely run for it, off to the Bahamas. I'd never win with the bank: they denied the insurance lapse on their part and wanted their money. More mobile melody as another possible enemy tried to get my attention. I didn't recognise the number and took the call.

'Iris, I need to speak to you. Please don't hang up.'

I hung up.

CHAPTER 14

I DIDN'T RECOGNISE HER to begin with and I was getting
good at voices. She could obviously disguise hers and she sounded
ordinary. Then she said it must be a lonely life on line.

'I can see you sitting in your room with the windows open,
hoping for a call you want and at the same time you don't. It's
a strain trying to pretend you can see the life of the unknown
person and at £1.50 a minute that person wants results. And
you're on your ownsome lonesome.' Was she opposite my flat
staring up at the open windows. I wanted to ask what kind of
windows I had and how many.

'Not like the old days. Goodnight, Isis, or is it Jesse?'

I was too shaken to take another call and immediately
phoned Starlight needing to tell her the whole story. Instead
I just mentioned a woman calling out of hours on my private
number. 'She can even get me right. I do sit alone in a room with
the window open.'

'Who doesn't? It's summer and we can hardly do our job in
a crowd.'

'She said how lonely it is.'

'Honey, no one wants to be a reader. Of course something's
gone wrong with our lives. This one is trying to pull you. You

get the occasional gay obsessive.'

'Dangerous?'

'Stalker. If she's got your private number she's got other things. You probably pass her in the street a dozen times.'

I didn't like that idea.

'What shall I do?'

'Call Sadie Chill. She has to look after you. That's her job.'

'Anything else?'

'Change your number.' She didn't think anymore of it and said goodbye. I guessed in her world it didn't amount to much.

Yes, I did feel lonely but Lou hadn't sounded that good herself. Flat and tired, but she had my private number, knew my past. The guru business at the Albert Hall wasn't satisfactorily explained away. Was the Isis sentence jumbled so the words fell together becoming simply coincidence and not a message? It was not a busy night, I waited an hour between calls and had lots of time to think scared thoughts. I tried to remember the first sheep call when she'd told me I was so good. It turned out I was so bad and that's what she was after. Of course she wouldn't touch Grey Owl. She could take me, a dumb newcomer and use me as she wanted. So what did she want? To put pressure from a supposedly spiritual source on a man for money and more. By my attitude she could tell certain things about me. I'd been around and I wasn't tripped up easily. I'd had the good life. When I didn't go for it why didn't she simply drop me? Was it because I knew too much? So she made sure she knew about me. She was pressurising me, playing with me, getting ready for the – whatever it was that followed. I didn't look forward to it.

And then it occurred to me she might once have been a reader on line.

*

I spent most of the long summer evenings looking out of the window. August was not a busy month for telephone psychics, and watching the activity on the street full of restaurants and pubs took my mind off unwanted subjects. I realised I was also looking for a particular person, a woman alone and interested in the house where I lived, even checking for names on the doorbells. Or a parked car with the occupant wearing shades. She would hide her eyes. Ordinary? Ugly? Fat? Nondescript? My mind felt happier with unique and elegant, a female beautifully made, standing out amongst the passers-by. She'd have dark hair, green or hazel long-lashed eyes. And then I saw Ray across the street talking to a woman who had her back to me, but I knew she wasn't a local. She was dressed casually, her body, what I could see of it, was toned and easeful. Even at this distance I could see she had allure. The hair was blond. Not so psychic there, Isis. It was tied back with small thin plaits hanging at the sides and she was smoking a cheroot. I knew the exact moment Ray saw me half hidden behind the blinds, because he casually turned the woman so she faced the street away from me and they started walking to the corner. Of course she'd got to him and as I suspected earlier had given him money. Her walk was graceful, effortless, she had presence and how my lover liked that. Could this encounter possibly get worse? Of course he was a star seeker. What else had attracted him to me in the good days? I was going to run down and follow them, even accost them, but the work phone rang and I had to make a decision. If I didn't pick up I'd be accused of missed calls and put further back in the queue or I'd be logged off and make nothing.

The caller, speaking from a public phone with plenty of background noise wanted to know if his woman was faithful or sleeping with his best friend and half the city. Drink came into it. His accent was thick and impossible. He didn't have enough money and the call was cut after two minutes. When I got to the window, Ray and the woman had gone.

Betty called and said the company was starting a promotion campaign across the UK. 'You should go for it because Howard said the money's good. Watch out tonight for a man in his thirties, well-spoken, goes by different names, Peter or Simon, but uses the same date of birth, 16 October 1972. He's an odd one. Just hang up if you get him and tell Howard.

What should I say to Ray? Nothing. Let's hear what he'd say to me. He brought back a good Indian takeaway and iced mint tea.

Later that night, I handed Ray the cards and said I'd read for him. 'Shuffle and cut in three and pick a pack. Surprisingly he didn't seem to mind. Had he nothing to hide? I spread out his chosen pile and brought the reading round to the blond girl with the attractive back view and cigar. He nodded quite happy to agree he'd seen her.

'I wanted to bring her up here so you could do her cards. She's got money.'

Of all the cover-ups he could give I felt this was the oddest – it was surreal. I asked where he'd met her.

'Met her? I know her. She plays chamber music.'

'I meant met her tonight.'

Did he sigh? The pause was a little too long. 'Coming out of Lemonia. I thought she'd fill an hour or so for you. She is fascinated by cards.'

So Lou was trying to get in. Not a stalker. That woman had too much self-value.

'Well, let's have her up.' I swept the cards back into a pack. I could see this wasn't going his way and he cleared away the curry boxes and turned on the television. I lowered the sound and wanted answers. I didn't need to be clairvoyant to know these conversations never did any good. By the end of it he said I was a jealous bitch and I maintained he was selling me out to an unknown blackmailer. I'd missed two calls and earned a black mark from Arnold. At 3 a.m. she was still a colleague in chamber music. Blackmailer known or not meant nothing to him.

* * *

If I took Ray off the list of Lou's collaborators it left Sadie Chill and Starlight. If I confronted them I'd be met with denial and then aggression. I agreed with my better judgement for once that it was ill-advised. I'd wait for Lou's next call.

Howard offered me the deal Betty had referred to. As a representative of The Line I'd introduce top clairvoyants at venues across the country. I didn't have to even consider this. However bad my career was at this time I'd still be recognised in the smaller places, the suburban towns around London, the cities up North. I'd be appearing at some of them in just over two months.

'It has to be no. Sorry, Howard.'

'You won't have to do the cards anymore.'

Another one who didn't think I was any good. And then he laid his ace. The pay wasn't quite up to Lou's rates, but better than being a telephone psychic.

Sadie Chill on next and if she didn't like rejection she wasn't showing it. She suggested I just try one gig but first meet her to talk through my career.

'What career?'

'Your psychic career, darling.' I felt she knew about the other one. Starlight would not have kept quiet about something she could use. Of course I still had pull in those places Sadie had chosen for the psychic presentations. All she had to do was encourage me to use my past success to enhance everyone's shaky present. She talked well about the benefits of unwanted change.

'I feel you're in a grey area. A wise ambivalence is not a bad thing. Think it over. No pressure whatever you decide. I love you.' How different she sounded to Lou.

I found watching Ray a strange occupation. During those long summer silences between mostly random callers I would see him crossing the street talking to the proprietor of the Italian restaurant, laughing in the pub garden, all light-hearted with the neighbours. Down-hearted began when he pushed open the door into my flat. So we had the conversation again that never got anywhere anyway. Who was the blonde woman?

'The same as she was when we last spoke about her.'

'Why lie?'

'Exactly.'

'But you were quite silent when I asked how you met her that evening. Outside Lemonia? I doubt it. Would that make you silent?'

He opened his arms wide and honestly. 'You're right. I did go quiet. It's the way you look at me. I think this stuff on line is truly bad for you. I felt scared not of you but for you. She is simply another musician. I did for a mad moment think she could be a client.'

'So what happened to that impulse?'

'I'm not sure that you're good enough.'

And then we laughed. Afterwards I nearly told him about Lou. My reticence showed me something. I still didn't unconditionally trust him. And then I got another idea. Maybe Lou was just a fan from the early days. Fans did unbelievable things.

CHAPTER 15

MIDDLE OF THE NIGHT, mobile ringing. Daytime bright Lou, all matter of fact: 'Do you know of the seer Mother Shipton? She made a prophecy about Primrose Hill.'

Was Mother Shipton on line? I couldn't place her. I was still half asleep.

'This is in the fifteenth century. "The hill stands firm and all around life in its many colours swirls until an end is found." So go and stand on the hill.'

'Why?' Awake and sitting up now.

'It's safe.'

Lou sounded casual, almost careless.

'The other way is do the smart thing. I've told you before. Tell him you see his grandmother. You're good on those.'

So she got people to ring me on line and listened in. I hadn't thought of that. In a failing reading grandmothers had been a safe bet.

'You just have to sit opposite him and get that heart chakra of his open. Do you know green is that chakra colour. Let's get some love going.'

'Why don't you do it?' Bad question but it was 4.30 dawn.

'I'll write a new prophecy for him and deliver it to you.

Learn it. He'll be at the hotel on the 18th. You'll be told which one and given the time. There's no more time, Jesse. Otherwise better get on top of that hill. Remember Mother Shipton. She also said "Primrose Hill shall be in centre hold a Bishop's see. And before that is done I shall be burned at the stake." And sing him "Ruby Red". He'll go for that.' She hung up and I couldn't sleep after that. Ray beside me pretended to sleep and then said, 'What is all that?'

I closed my eyes and counted sheep.

My nerves were stretched to the edge of panic as the next afternoon I walked along the side of Primrose Hill. I felt she could be at the top watching me. I went into the bookshop and asked if they had a copy of Mother Shipton's prophecy. The bookseller knew of it. And then a woman behind the fiction shelf started to recite what I took to be the prophecy. '"It shall be on centre hold, a Bishop's see."' She paused. 'That's a meeting place for a divine plan.'

This could be no other than Lou. I ran into the street, towards the canal, pounding out all the injustice of the past months. A convertible passed me and the woman wore shades and long scarves flowing, and she turned and whistled as I ran. Lou would do that. The canal's narrow path was choked with people. A woman had fallen in. The atmosphere was not hopeful. Not wanting to look at what the paramedics were doing, I ran into Camden Market and Starlight was suddenly beside me. 'Hey, it's not that bad.' And she took hold of me quite fiercely. 'This needs a drink.' Starlight looked after me for the rest of the day. She even checked if a message had been put through my front door. It was the mention of Primrose Hill, the way the adversary had brought it in that so upset me. Primrose Hill was safe, the one bright place. Starlight said I should not go on line that night and bought me food and drinks and took me to her place to wash and rest. She knew some of it, perhaps most but didn't ask questions. All she'd say was: 'You've had a good run with music, so use it. Let Sadie Chill give it the works and you'll be up again.'

'Did you tell Sadie about me?' I knew she had and that she'd deny it.

'Be smart, Jesse. Let people take care of you. She'll resurrect you.' I remembered to thank her for the care she'd shown.

'We're all in this together. Any of us can have a bad punter. I'm going to take you to Kit. That's who I always go to. She'll sort you out. She used to be a model.'

*

The old house in Kentish Town with the blinds drawn in the pale evening light and the grandfather clock mute in the hallway belonged to another time. An original stained glass window on the first floor landing let in the last of the light colourfully. The house was untouched through lack of money or design and built in the days when they knew how to build houses. The staircase was generous, the banister cool to the touch as we started to climb to what Starlight called 'the boudoir'. The backdoor was open allowing in a soft breeze and I could see part of an original Victorian garden overgrown with a curving stone wall at the end. I stood still to fully take in this atmosphere unknown in the present day. It was as though the house held onto all that had happened here and the air was alive with reactivated moments refusing to fade. A real clairvoyant would read its atmosphere before reaching even the staircase. It must have been a joyful place, had housed love and in return been loved itself. Good people had lived here. I could hear the shiver of the leaves from the sycamore tree. Did it like me pick up the presence of memories too precious to let die? Distinct perfume now, 'Sweet Figs of Amalfi'. Undeniably.

'I always feel better when I come here.' Starlight kept her voice low and we paused to look at the garden. 'It's like a good parent and I feel included here, even loved.'

I asked about the perfume which I'd know anywhere. She hadn't noticed perfume. I asked who'd lived here, my voice also dropping. I knew the atmosphere we both appreciated came from an earlier epoch and had nothing to do with today. She said well to do people had owned the house because there were servants' rooms in the attic. She called to a man eating downstairs in the kitchen. 'Just going up, Jack.'

He lifted a fork in agreement and a black and white collie-cross ran in from the garden. Starlight greeted the dog and it watched with eyes not unlike hers, which since I'd first seen her seemed closer together than ever.

'They're a good crowd,' she said. 'Kit's a right person.' She checked her appearance in a small pocket mirror and satisfied shook back her hair. I thought the pause that came next was a little nervous and then she opened a heavy wooden door into a room which held only darkness. 'This is the salon. Kit's in here. 'The sweet Figs of Amalfi' perfume was strong, and I waited for her to turn on a light. I hadn't expected the darkness and probably would not normally have entered the room but nothing was normal these days. Then I heard soft voices rising and falling calmly and as I became accustomed to the room the darkness paled to half light and I could make out a small group of women by the far wall.

'So you're the new messenger from Sirius. Welcome.' And a tall woman moved effortlessly towards us, the boyish hips swaying naturally. The room now had dimensions and forms and was graceful with high, moulded ceilings and sofas around the walls.

'Why Sirius?' I asked.

'Because Sirius gave us what we needed to know and we became intelligent beings.' She talked as though she believed it. I didn't know if she meant us in the room or the planet in general.

Still not able to see properly, I stayed where I was. Then the shutters were pulled back and the blue hour became visible through the large open window. The woman's hand was well made and strong as she took mine, her eyes light and curious without being intrusive. Her voice was smoky and sure as she

asked if I'd prefer tea with lemon or mint. This was Kit, the one
to come to in times of trouble. She kept hold of my hand and
led me forward. 'This room keeps hold of its darkness.' Was she
reading my mind? 'It loves mystery. So do we.' She drew on a long
thin cigarette in a black holder and looked out into the nostalgic
blue of the oncoming night. 'We'll see the moon alright.'

An elderly elegant man in a smoking jacket half lay on a
chaise longue. He, too, was looking at the sky.

'We like to see the stars as they become apparent. After all
they're our friends,' and Kit pointed to the first one visible.
'That's Venus. It should be good for you.'

There were now enough lighted candles and sweetly coloured
lamps to create a tangible atmosphere, more powerful than the
one shut out outside. That got on by itself in the unfolding of
modern uncertainty. This room, the salon, belonged to a sure
time that would not be allowed to escape, to fade. Even the
music, the clothes, the objects were from earlier times. They had
been expecting me. Kit said, while sitting in a circle, my arrival
had been predicted and the other women, three of them, agreed
my showing up was fortuitous. I was given a cooling herbal tea
and the most comfortable sofa and they sat close around me,
their eyes welcoming, prepared to trust, to heal.

The light ball on the ceiling was switched on and turned
slowly creating the broken confetti effect of a fifties dance hall.
Much of the room was from the fifties and the women dressed
up, I realised, in celebration of that era. Around the walls old
black and white photos and posters of performers and celebrities
from the past. The fifties phones were heavy and black with
the early numbers and codes: 'Latimer', 'Juniper', 'Flaxman',
'Primrose' followed by four digits. Just visible in the distance
screens and card tables, a wireless set, an open fireplace.

I remembered Kit from magazines twenty years ago. She
had been a well-known model and must now be in her early
fifties. She held herself beautifully her body supple and thin and
it seemed to defy any possibility of voluptuousness. The black

Chanel dress, the slender tapering high-heeled shoes, the long earrings fitted perfectly the image she wanted to create. It was simple, authentic and would be acceptable at any place, any time. The other women endeavoured to copy her but her style was elusive, her make-up lavish enough made her beautiful. The platinum blonde hair swept back at the sides boyishly in what they used to call a DA would draw attention anywhere. She was got up to go out on the town somewhere significant and glamorous, a dinner or a club. She was in fact going on line. 'Ten every night unless I go to private clients.' She fitted another cigarette into the holder.

'But you're all dressed up to go out.' I thought her evening had been cancelled.

'I'd dress up to stay in.'

The tape was changed and The Platters singing 'Only You' pleased everyone. It was too good to talk through and Kit moved enjoying the rhythm, easy in her body. I was offered fruit from one of the many bowls and sparkling mineral water with lemon. It all looked clean and fresh, but in this light I couldn't tell about the room, how dusty or worn out it was. The song came to an end and Kit did the talking.

'We know who you are, Jesse, and it's good to have you here. Firstly I love your music and we've got all your recordings. I pick up you're feeling a victim yet you're stronger than the one who hides in the spotlight. You wouldn't find her in a room like this.' The women laughed. I couldn't see Starlight. 'Tell us what you suppose we don't know.'

I said what I knew and it didn't take long.

'You are sad because you think your life as a singer is over. It's going through a transition. It will never be over because you're meant to sing. You'll go back into an earlier style and bring that music into our lives. It needs to happen.'

I thought of Ray's suggestion I sing in French the old songs.

'You'll know it when it finds you.' She turned to the man half seen in the corner. 'What do you think, Elmore?'

His voice was rich and deep. 'You've had a career. The public know you. This woman Lou could be from that time. An admirer of yours. And now she thinks it's an opportune moment to reach you. You have no idea how much you have affected people's lives.'

Starlight spoke next. She was back in the darkness. 'I hadn't thought of it, but . . .'

'Don't go on thinking of it,' said Kit. 'It doesn't fit what I'm hearing. The woman had no idea when she first phoned who you were. She just wanted a player who could handle things, who she in turn could handle.' She looked at me, more looked into me deeply, disturbingly. 'She was searching for on the skids with class, a broken down career even better, so you'd do what she wanted. Why didn't you do it? You'd both make a bit out of it.'

The others agreed with me that it was dangerous. 'Big, bigger than you think. They won't let you go once you know too much. But you are well protected.' Kit looked around the edges of my bodily outline. 'I'm glancing at your aura. A little shattered. You need healing. Your aura shows you have an Egyptian guide. I like that. Do the work for Sadie and really go behind it. It'll start you back on your career.'

The half light suited these people, made them look young and flawless, presumably how they wanted to be. Kit sprayed herself with the fifties perfume 'Je Revien', powdered her face and picked up a black phone. 'Have to log on,' and she dialled this instrument from forty years ago, its number Cunningham 1971. She wore serious jewellery. What was she doing working for Sadie Chill?

'Do you really dress up like this just to go on line?'

'But of course.'

'Why?'

'It's who I am.'

And she took her first call. The others were quite mesmerised watching her. Elmere kept the music soft. She handled her information beautifully. No hang-ups there. She spoke as though giving the caller something unique. At the end she said as though having passed on something of great value: 'That is all I can give you. I hope it's of help.' Chime. Phone down. Yes, she had value and in turn dispensed it.

CHAPTER 16

THE NEXT MORNING I decided to revisit Kit but, once in the Kentish Town area, could not find the house. I phoned Starlight who asked what I wanted and I said a reading. She said Kit only worked at night.

'Maybe, but I still need the address.'

She was undeniably giving me wrong directions when I recognised the sycamore tree and sloping wall.

Starlight said they never went out in the day and I asked why not. 'The night suits them. They find today's expectations just not worth it. They make their own.'

'Is it their house?'

'Jack owns it but has no money to do it up. They rent it from him. He used to be a photographer. That's how he met Kit when she was modelling. He still works now and then.' She told me I'd never get inside the house and at that moment Jack came down Dunollie Road, walking the Collie dog, and said Kit was awake and having coffee in the garden.

I tried to climb on to the curving wall at the back. Jumping up I could see Kit sitting on an old deck chair, eyes closed. I got a better grip on the wall and called to her. She did for a moment seem undecided, and asked why I didn't come in the usual way.

Because she'd be unlikely to let me in. She put on sunglasses, made a decision and started towards the backdoor. Without make-up she looked old, her face surprisingly lined. She took me upstairs to the room next to the salon, an intimate space from where came the smell of 'Figs of Amalfi' and over the years had collected atmospheres so thick I felt I was sinking in someone else's reality. This room, the boudoir, was the beating heart of the house. She gathered clothes off a couch and said I should sit down. I was more interested in the rails of irreplaceable items she'd modelled in the fifties and sixties, Balenciaga, Jacques Fath, Chanel, Worth. Furs, swagger coats, platform-heeled shoes, ballerina pumps, suede lace-up boots in lilac, others in pink, everything brushed and cleaned and kept perfectly. In the far corner an upright piano piled with sheet music. The dressing table was spread with make-up and perfumes, their bottles reminiscent of a time of undeniable glamour. The make-up containers were over thirty years old, Coty, Snowfire vanishing cream, Velouty cream powder, Leichner theatre make-up, Bourgois rouge, Helena Rubinstein toilet waters and perfume sticks. Even in that crowded space there were collections of photographs, postcards, theatre programmes, magazines. She wound up the portable record player and chose a French song. 'Le Mer.' I picked up an empty bottle of 'Californian Poppy' and Kit said the working girls used to wear that in the forties and fifties. It had been sold in Woolworths at one shilling and three pence. The bottle was dried out but there remained a lingering scent of a summer long since gone.

Quickly she made up her face, smearing on gels and creams and was transformed. It could be any hour in that boudoir and no unwanted dreary daylight was remembered here.

'You live in another time,' I said.

'And we keep it that way. Why should we leave an era we love and be dragged into something out there that has no value for us. We like the Blue Hour.' She pointed to Guerlain's scent of the same name.

'There is free will and that sounds crazy coming from someone who spends every night with people who want the opposite. It's all written at birth. The blue print of our destiny. It's in your palm. But the free will comes in the way you choose to see it, and deal with it.'

I asked about her work on line, how she'd started, why she did it. I still had the feeling she had serious money.

'Why do you dress up? They can't see you.' Did it intensify her skill?

'Why should I look terrible because I work on line?'

She invited me for a walk on Hampstead Heath, went to the piano and lifted the lid. The inside was stuffed with money and she took out a handful of twenties. 'We'll have lunch.'

As I went out a magazine caught my attention and I tried to see the date.

'The fifties again,' she said. 'You're attracted to that time. I wonder why?'

'Oh, it's a style thing.' I dismissed it. I had enough to worry about.

She looked at me, not without a certain concern and said, 'I still wonder why.'

＊

We ate lunch at an Italian restaurant at the bottom of Swains Lane opposite the Heath. Suddenly I could feel the shadow of the debt mountain and I hunched over, held the table. 'I need help.' My voice was small.

'Of course you do.' She spoke calmly. 'And Sadie is the one person who will give it to you. Go to the one who has power. There's no good running to people like Star or me. You need a company behind you. Be valuable to them and they'll take care of you. They'll have enough resource to match the enemy.'

'What do I have to do?'

'Present the new show. Introduce the star mediums. Give them a song or two. Get behind it. Then they'll not want you messed about with. If you go on sitting by the phone waiting for clients that you can't handle anyway you become weak and not necessary to the company. You're not a natural clairvoyant. To keep a reading going must sometimes be a nightmare.'

She crossed the Heath with long easy strides towards Kite Hill with its view of London, not as good as from Primrose Hill, and I remembered Lou's prediction and shivered.

I asked what she thought of Lou's persistence.

'The target, whoever he is, has heard your voice so she thinks she has to use you. She's built you up as the carrier of spirit messages for him so she can't pull in someone else. You have a memorable voice. When you get on the show and back to the performer you really are this person, whoever she is, will realise you're out of reach. You're no longer the victim trying to eke out an existence. She'll have to find someone else.'

As we sat on the hill I asked about her past.

'The thing about being psychic no one has to know your past as long as you know their future.'

Then she talked a little about her modelling career and how she loved Coco Chanel and the little black dress. And Ungaro with the mathematical lines as though from out of space. She'd done well for Jacques Fath and took his fifties swagger coat into the sixties. That made her remember his best model Florence. 'The wife kept the power.'

'Jealous?'

'God, no. Jacques was gay. The wife chose to run things and we used to go in a group to Deauville which was always fashionable. Later I went there with the French singer Serge Gainsbourg and his English wife.' Suddenly she got up and needed to hurry. She always had a private yoga class in the afternoon followed by a massage. Kit was disciplined, almost ritualistic and decided on solutions and the most practical way to arrive at them. She wanted me to ring Sadie Chill from her phone and I wondered if she would get some kudos. Did she sense what I was thinking? She said, 'You can't go to the police with that story. Where's the crime? The blood on the carpet? That's what they need. They'll just dismiss you as strange. Well it is a strange business we're in. They'll tell you to find the villain yourself if you're so psychic.'

In the daylight she sometimes looked a little lost like a child not knowing the territory. She blinked at the sun and didn't altogether like it, or the traffic sounds, or the bestial noise of the junior school let out for afternoon break on Parliament Hill. Daylight gave her the wrong kind of shadows. She needed the night to put on her best colours.

*

I didn't feel safe going home and sat in the boudoir playing ballads from those earlier years on the wind-up gramophone from the thirties. She had an assortment of old recordings on 78s, big black circular discs that scratched easily and were breakable. And then smaller ones, EPs that arrived in the fifties, and I remembered my grandfather's collection in colourful cardboard sleeves. The quality of the sound was dependent on frequently changing the needle and Kit had few left. Most of the collection was signed, Johnny Ray, Frankie Laine, Sinatra, Mario Lanza, The Ink Spots, and the French singers: Piaf, Trenet, Halliday. Photos of the fashion shows, the balls, premieres, clubs, and racing events were pinned across the far wall and around the mirror. Her collection of magazines recorded a world to which I felt I would have belonged. The boudoir was the core of this woman and every item saved randomly added to her essence. Nothing was hidden, everything on show. I would have liked to know about her life but I didn't think I was going to get that. From the magazines I learned she'd been married twice to wealthy men and lived a fashionable monied life between New York, Las Vegas, Paris, London, Deaville, Baden-Baden. The smell of her perfumes and powders allowed me into another time which could still be activated in this precious room. Her sudden drop from fame was not explained, nothing in the magazines. She'd simply dropped out. When I asked what had happened she said, 'I got old.'

Daylight let me see the house for what it was and it showed up the years of wear. Its mood was quite different and ransacked of all that had made it mysterious the previous night.

Starlight had been back to my flat and there was no envelope from Lou. Just bills. She told me to do the Sadie gig and buy myself some good will. The truth – I was classier than any gig of Sadie's, but that was better not mentioned. The church clock chimed beautifully and we were now into the Blue Hour.

I said I was amazed someone with Kit's past had ended up on line.

'Well, look at you. The victim of a woman who wants you to do something in a hotel with a possible husband and tarot cards. Deadly. Don't touch it. And Kit is much, much more and you can't imagine what goes on here. She's a High Priestess and teaches divination. She develops mediums – Grey Owl came here.'

So it was an academy for psychics. I looked at the solid comforting house and overgrown unspoiled garden, the ivy creeping walls, the spacious rooms, high ceilings, elegance. It fitted the subject.

'They have evenings of magic and Theosophy, and the works of Anna Blavatsky and Alice Bailey. They free trapped souls that can't reach spirit. Elmore does a show of hand shadows.'

I didn't get a chance to ask what that was because she was eager to keep speaking and impress me. 'Elmore can speak in voices.'

'From the fifties?'

'Much earlier. The 1850s. He can bring through Edgar Cayce.'

I hoped I looked impressed. I didn't know who Edgar Cayce was.

'After all these people can transform matter. They can take us back to Ancient Egypt.'

I was impressed. If life got any worse that might be my destination.

I was called up to the salon, and Kit, sitting behind a card table, indicated I take a chair opposite. Elmore, wearing a three-piece velvet suit, played a violin and I recognised the once popular tune, hackneyed and over-rich with romance, a favourite in my grandfather's time. Elmore gave it even more and it dipped and soared almost unbearably. It shook to an end and Elmore placed the violin on the chaise-longue. 'It's a piece everyone knew but none the worse for that – "Ah, Sweet Mystery of Life" – Mischa Elman played it at our first . . .' A look from Kit stopped him talking.

'Elmore is a Renaissance man,' Kit said, off-hand.

'What's that?' Starlight was in the room.

'A man of all trades.'

It didn't sound like an insult.

She gave me a thin pack of long, narrow cards like Gothic doorways. 'Shuffle.' They were hard to handle. 'Cut with your left hand.' She laid them out in three rows. These were not the tarot designs I was used to. 'I was born on the right side of the tracks but couldn't wait to get to the wrong side.' She looked at me and I at her. 'What does that mean to you?'

It didn't mean anything. Yes, it was familiar.

'You're in something that requires action. You have to calmly get out.' And again she pushed the boat out for Sadie Chill and I'd be doing the tour better than I could imagine. She folded the cards away and I thought that was it, but she picked up an ordinary pack of playing cards, chose 21 and shuffled. 'I'm going to do something I haven't done for a long time. No one has – "The Grand Star".'

'That's an old one,' said Elmore.

'21 cards, always 21.' She laid them in a circular pattern, tapped the table and I thought of her earlier remark about the wrong side of the tracks. Who had said that? Kit tapped the table, impatient now. 'It won't come out,' and she looked at Elmore.

He tapped on the floor with his cane. The sound had a sense of consequence to it, a message. I felt it was taking me to a further reality, hypnotically taking my mind.

'You don't have to be afraid,' said Kit, matter-of-fact, and I supposed I didn't.

Elmore looked across the table as the cane went on with its rhythmic tapping. Pointing with his other hand at her circle, he said, 'I see 10 of Hearts. Remember it counteracts the evil.'

'So there is evil there.' I was up off the chair leaning over, trying to make sense of what was there.

'Sit down,' said Kit, and she had authority because I sat automatically. 'Don't bother trying to look at the cards. You won't understand them.' She beckoned Elmore to join her. 'It's covered. Hard to see. It's the . . .' She paused, surprised, and waited for his interpretation.

'"The Seraphim's Stratagem". I'd say she who hides in the spotlight is well guarded.'

'What can you see?' I asked. How often was I going to be frightened? I'd been more frightened while doing this job than at any other time in my adult life.

'Reflections. On and on,' said Kit.

'Yes, the creature is well protected.' Elmore lifted up the Queen of Wands. 'She's a chameleon. Almost flawless. She doesn't leave tracks.' He put the card back in its place. 'She's a bad enemy because she's got all manner of deception. Corridors of reflections.' He put a hand on my shoulder. 'We'll track her down.'

'But I don't know her.' As though that helped.

Kit looked up briefly. 'Oh, you have known her once.' And she folded the cards and shuffled them. I was thinking back into the past searching for 'the once'. She said I should ask a question. The 'once' needed all my attention. Was 'once' one time or back in time?

'Am I safe?'

She flung up her hands. 'You've been given the way out.'

'Any other?'

'Yes, keep sitting waiting for calls and hoping it's not her.'

I asked what she got on her.

'Very defended. Hard to read. Will reinvent herself to get

what she wants. Another question?'

I wanted to ask if Ray was in this, but asked if he knew her. She looked at the cards and shook her blonde head slowly. I realised how well made she was and the hair stylish and just right. 'Is he faithful?' That was less bad than the previous question. She gathered the 21 ordinary playing cards. 'Have you a real cause for jealousy? If the 7 of Diamonds comes out in the first 15 cards, yes.' She started laying cards and I feared what I'd see. No 7 of Diamonds. 'I've never seen a reading like that,' I said.

'Oh, these are the business. The old style!' She closed the pack and I felt she'd seen something that disquieted her.

Starlight poured us glasses of iced tea and, without reason, I asked her if there had been anything else in the post. I suppose I was thinking of my tour and any contracts that were ready to sign.

'Only something, an ad about sheepskin. Was it coats reduced?' I understood all bets were off. 'Was it a card? A flier? Something put through everyone's door?' My mouth was dry.

She was trying to remember. 'It had a picture of a sheep.' She was triumphant.

Kit gave me a long look.

I reached for the phone. Yes, all bets were off.

The deal was simple. Sadie Chill gave me the schedule, the local TV dates, the money. As she'd said it was an improvement on line reader. 'And then you'll go on Sky. You'll get to like it,' she promised.

I asked how long I'd be on tour, and she said why stop? It just went on and on and then started from the beginning again. I'd front competitions for local newcomers to the psychic line. I'd host corporate evenings. I'd present the ten-minute documentary on palm reading. I'd sing the theme song. I'd use my real name.

'I'm not making a career of it,' I replied, surprised how sharp I sounded.

She called me back and said Howard would make the arrangements. Kit took the phone and talked softly about other things and long enough for Sadie to understand who had persuaded and finally delivered the new star. Kit would even choose my clothes. Then I made my mistake and told Starlight how much I was getting and she did try to hide – was it anger?

'Well, Lady Luck has certainly turned things around. Or was it a sheep?'

Kit told me to wait in the garden while she prepared the evening programme. I started downstairs and then got drawn into the boudoir. I opened the crinkle cut glass bottle of 'Chantilly' by Houbigant and inhaled deeply. I kept my nose over the bottle drawing in the life of the perfume. It lifted the sadness, anaesthetised the pain. Would I ever get back to the lovely time when I sang amazing music? The disappointment made me actually choke. The power of smell, it evoked immediately an era, a lost love, a first school. There was nothing as evocative as smell. Wood smoke was the strongest and most nostalgic. Then I heard Starlight's voice hissing with anger. 'Why should she get the breaks? She's not even committed to the work.' Her voice changed and became sarcastic as she imitated me, 'I'm not making a career of it.'

'Don't worry what she says.' Kit spoke smoothly. 'Don't they all say they're in the racket for the time being? Only temporary. And don't they all stay put? By the time they've shuffled a Marseilles tarot pack so the cards start to wear they're in for good. It gets to them – the hours – the sloth – the dodges. They can milk it a dozen ways. They crawl out of bed in the afternoon over to the couch and start making money. It's small money but easy money, and bit by bit they're finished as far as routine goes. And there's something about working at night. It's mystical, attractive. Anything can happen. Once they're in they're in.' Kit sounded quite different, a little hard, cynical. Was she talking about herself?

Starlight caught me up as I walked along the canal. She said she was glad for me. I knew Kit had sent her as I might have agreed to the deal, but nothing was signed.

'Kit's glad too.'

'She sure sounded it.' I let Starlight get what she could out of that.

'You don't want to pick on Kit. She has a high-born guide that speaks through her. Kit's face changes and another person appears.' She sounded proud of Kit.

'How?'

'It rises to the surface. When this happens the group goes into deep attunement and time travel. They reached a star near Sirius which was lost and near destruction and it appeared here in Kit's occult table. It was minute but gave off huge yellow light in blasts. That's how I got my name because I was there when it happened.'

It seemed Starlight was included in some of the special ceremonies and I wondered what the others thought of her aspirations to not reach a distant planet, but the sexual predilections of men and women on this one. Did they know?

She did hesitate. 'It's part of life. They know that.'

It's a racket. I knew that.

✳

The sheepskin leaflet was amongst riffraff in the hall waiting to be thrown out. Normally I wouldn't even notice it. The sheep design was hardly menacing. Did other houses in the street have a copy? I tried my neighbour's but the hallway was swept and clear. The house opposite with its untidy entrance and cluttered hallway had two leaflets and, relieved, I went home.

The agent said my bookings for my tour were better up north. How bad were they down south? He thought once the CD got going there would be more response. Ray had put out a well-designed packaging and the distribution was fair. Not one adjective made me hopeful.

'Level with me.'

'It's not "Ruby Red",' he said.

So I was in for the psychic tour. It seemed I'd have no trouble meeting that expectation. Before going to bed I was back on line: once you're in you're in. Vinnie after a night out asking me to get a cab for a one-to-one in person. As the High Priestess of tarot had said, you can milk it a dozen ways.

*

I had that dream again. Ray wasn't beside me and for a moment I couldn't remember if he was on tour. The dream still filled my thoughts and it had an inevitability making clear there would be no way of changing the order of things. It replayed, just to make sure, first the scream, then the sound of the body falling hard onto the road. I thought that was all and was about to hurry away. Then I saw a slippery thing rolling towards the kerb. It was an eyeball.

The dream hadn't changed since its first performance back in childhood. And then for years it was gone.

CHAPTER 17

THE FIRST GIG WAS Oxford and I took the train from Paddington on this cool beautifully bright day, far from the ruthless heat of August. I carried my script, my scarlet dress in the light leather bag I'd last used for New York. The money, bank cards and phone were tight in a pouch around my waist. I was over-aware of my possessions as though they were threatened. An item could be mislaid or perhaps stolen.

Although most seats were free the person who got on just before the train left the station walked through the long, narrow carriage to my section at the far end and chose the seat directly opposite mine so taking away any sense of privacy. I was irritated, more so as this intruder seemed to command attention. I was looking out of the window and had not really taken her in. I knew it was a woman, I could smell the perfume. I was about to ask why she had to push her way into my space when there were so many seats available. Of course I'd have to move and automatically picked up the leather bag. And then I noticed her shoes, high-heeled, exceptionally well designed. Her ankles were long and fine and I followed them up to the calves in the tanned gossamer stockings. I had to look again at the thighs, the waist, all flowing lines, long and undeniably elegant, as she rested easily in the corner of her seat. She was well made, a model or a dancer. I lifted my attention above the breasts discreet in the high fashion silk top and her eyes were waiting for mine. Green eyes, those of a cat, long-lashed, slanted at the corners, slightly amused. Her mouth was exceptional. I thought it was the most beautiful mouth I had ever seen. The lips were etched in a fine perfect symmetry, not too full. They were wonderfully alive, the focus of the face. The dark, lustrous hair was gathered up in a chignon at the back of her head, a little wild like a bird's nest. I thought she was too special by far to be sitting in a second class train carriage on the way to Slough. She belonged on a film set, in a fashion shoot, in the life of a wealthy respected man. The long lines of her body arrived by courtesy of generations of well-made forebears allowed her distinction. Her eyes no longer connected with mine as she looked into a distance known only to her, not without certain nostalgia and longing. I watched this person without choice and could not get enough of her beauty and the secret beauty she beheld. She must be a movie actress, I decided. But how many had this breeding and charisma? I kept hold of my bag, drew it close to me. I must have foreseen something undesirable was about to happen. Maybe I could after all see into the future. She opened her lips and words came through them and I'd know that voice anywhere. She may look as though overtaken by the onrush of remembered passion, romantic, wistful Cathy in Wuthering Heights, longing for Heathcliff, but the voice could not be more different. City tough, as she said: 'How are the sheep doing?' The laugh was tough too.

Of course I'd clung to my small luggage, frightened. How could she be here? She should not be here. Trying for time, I looked at the window but didn't see the passing countryside. I saw instead her reflection in the glass on and on indefinitely, a passage of reflections, imprisoning, no escape here and I remembered Elmore as he tried to locate her. Defended was the word. Reflected over and over again. The Seraphim's Stratagem. She'd got me. She was here. It did not bode well. Yet she was beautiful. I turned and looked directly at her face. Beautiful and unearthly.

A voice now, inside me and private. 'Play it carefully, Isis.' The voice I used for clients giving advice. 'Let her do the talking.'

Then she spoke. 'You're going to have to start using your brain, Isis. Forget about feeding the lovelorn with the wrong kind of hope. Just get my husband believing in redemption.'

'He isn't your husband.' Shouldn't have said it.

'Of course not, Isis. We've already done that.' She now had the control with me she needed. 'You just shuffle a pack of cards and tell him what you see. No sweat there. You'll see what I tell you to see.'

I didn't like her tone.

'When is this exactly?'

'Tonight exactly.'

'Why am I doing it?'

'You're too far in it.'

The train swung so the sun came on the other side and for a moment the woman seemed insubstantial as though made up of light. Shadow gave her back her flesh. She looked amused. Reading thoughts?

'But I don't know anything about it.'

Did she sigh? 'You're in it.'

I didn't like the sound of that. She was stirred up and ready to act. How I hoped it was to get off the train at Slough. We were coming into the station and I did think she might be reading my thoughts because she laughed and her teeth seemed pointed like a rodent's and the beauty was quite gone. It must have been the way the light fell.

'You think you're not going to do it. I'm no clairvoyant, but I bet you'll be sitting in a Park Lane hotel around 11 o'clock tonight.' The teeth again, jagged as though broken.

I didn't answer. I had no answer.

'Remember Rome?'

Rome. Now she had the high ground. I'd sung in that city in the good days.

'You were quite the party girl, so they say.'

'I'll be in Oxford doing a gig at 11 tonight.' I got up and started to move to another seat.

'There was a girl, a model from the Ford agency. Top of the heap.' She carried on talking softly, confident I would stay and listen. I was listening. She spoke as though telling a story and I had no idea where she was going with this but it seemed to be designed to place me in the hotel she'd just mentioned without fail at 11 p.m. that night.

'She was doing a fashion shoot for one of the glossies, and Ricco from the Stephano family was keen on her. Of course he was Mafia. Most of the guys were. Sinatra was there and Dean and Eddie Fisher, and Ricco gave a party. All the models and starlets currently in town were brought in for decoration and there was a pile of coke like a wedding cake on every table. And the music was tops. Sinatra's lot made it a fabulous night.'

I was still listening and I felt the familiar psychic chill. A pause for me to ask a question. No questions.

'You remember the Ford Agency? New York. The best. The model was all set for a career. And the party ended as even those parties do and there was just Ricco and a couple of associates and the model. He wanted her. That's why he threw the party. And there were a couple of girls left over. The coke was the best. You know how it is.'

I did. I didn't.

'And then someone murdered Ricco.' She allowed a pause. It meant nothing to me. 'Now, Jesse, you remember that.'

She waited for me to remember.

'But that was years ago.' Had it been in the papers? Ricco from the Stephano family. Had I read about it?

'Just one model, two assistants and some girls too out of it to leave, too pissed to do much. Could they even tell if someone was dead? The cops were called and when they eventually came to the mansion once owned by the Borghese family there was one girl left. And Ricco of course. He wasn't going anywhere.'

She invited me to sit in my seat. Were we only at Reading?

'So who did it?' she asked.

The train was now crowded with back-packers from a festival. And she had to shout the next bit. 'So who do you think shot Ricco Stephano dead?'

We sat in our own silence with the babble around us ignored. Then she spoke. 'It certainly was no sheep.'

Stunned, I kept my eyes away from her. The window showed me only too many reflections of Lou.

'Not psychic now?' she asked, tauntingly. 'They said it was a Mafia killing. It seemed to suit everyone to keep it that way.'

Now I did remember something of the crime. Movie-stars had been present and politicians, and then it was hushed up. I was just starting my career. 'It was years ago,' I said again.

'Oh, don't give away your age. You were a fun girl in those days. Plenty saw your public performance and a few the one afterwards. Even Ricco said you were wild.'

I needed time. I needed to make myself safe. 'I was never there.'

'In blackout you were. You liked the nose candy.'

So a crime syndicate was going to set me up. Was the only option to continue as their messenger? For a terrible moment I did wonder if I had been at the murder scene. I had done my share of parties and the trimmings.

She started listing the producers and backers of my shows, all those years ago in Rome. I was quiet too long because I was trying to remember the dates, the years. Over fifteen years ago, nearer twenty. New, at the beginning of everything, each night was a night out and I was on everyone's party list.

'So what was this mansion like?' I tried to keep my face neutral. Of course I could get her on a blackmail charge.

'Oh, the usual pile of old stones. It had a nice front but a terrible door. A red door.'

Worse and worse. Not Tunbridge Wells then? I should get my money back. 'So who was the model?' As if I didn't know.

'You're looking at her.'

Yes, I did my share of parties and stopped the drink and drugs before thirty, like a lot of the music set. Did I have blackouts? I was sure having one now. I needed time and quiet, a sweet tea for shock. I remembered Kit looking at the cards. 'You have known her once.' Didcot Parkway next stop.

She leaned towards me, her cat's eyes without expression. 'You were well out of it that night. Did someone put you up to it? The Ricco thing. Or were you jealous? Maybe you liked the dude? Shame there wasn't only you and him left. Three's a crowd. And I was deadly sober. I never use.' The train slowed into the station. 'But every blackout has a bright awakening. All you've got to do is be psychic and let me be the guide.'

I did try to get control. 'It's a long time ago. If I'd been involved I'd know about it. The police . . .'

She spoke quickly as the train slowed. 'I agree it's a long time ago. Forget the police. They're an illusion. Just think not everyone was happy he was murdered. He's Italian. He has a family. Your way out is my husband. The poor creature hopes there's an after-world. Just say the lines and keep seeing sheep.'

She got up and left the train at Didcot.

*

I didn't get off the train as she might have expected, but sat ripped to bits, skinned in the emptying carriage, her voice with its taunting questions still reverberating in my head, the sound unable to leave and finally wearing out as the train started its own set of noise. I wasn't sure she had got off at Didcot but simply walked along the platform to a different carriage. She'd be there at Oxford, hidden, and so able to make these sudden appearances. She belonged in darkness. 'So who killed him? Not psychic now?' she mocked. She was implying I'd killed him? An accusation. A revelation. It was the last thing I could have expected, topping everything in this lean, grim time. Whatever kind of night it had been, surely a party trick on this scale would be beyond forgetting. Yet I didn't remember the man or the crime. How had he died? Had she mentioned that? She'd said 'shot'. I'd heard of a drug-taker coming down from weeks of using, not sure whether the body beside him in the bed or the next room, or the garden, was dead or even there. He was so out of it he had to wait until sober to discover a corpse or hallucination and, if dead, under what circumstances. I'd certainly done my share of parties in the old days and was no stranger to a line of coke, but nothing inside me that the drugs or drink could inflame would kill or want to kill. Nothing was angry or violent enough for that act. Of that I was sure yet I hadn't been able to stand my ground and fight her back. I'd taken a drink, rolled a spliff but my career always came first. Yet the murder in Rome had sounded familiar. Was it something in the newspapers? Was it the way she told it? When I didn't get off the train at Didcot she'd expect me to carry on to Oxford, then turn around on the first fast train back to London, too upset, too frightened to do the venue. I'd be hunting down past agents, producers and witnesses at that party scene. I'd be phoning Rome needing journalists, the police, trying to get at the truth. I'd certainly be reading cards in a red dress for an unknown client at eleven that evening, properly obedient, terrified into a state almost amiable. She was certain of that. I'd need her. I was hers.

One piece of advice kept me at the small town outside Oxford: 'Be valuable to the company and they'll look after you.' Kit's words stayed with me through that terrible day and kept me on stage doing what I always did. The show was live and the psychic performance simple enough and I just followed the cues and 'stood it up on its feet' as they said in the business. 'An Ace red, a love bed. Two Jacks and a King, not a good thing. Two Aces and a 9 of Cups. With Kings this lovely lady sups.' That made me think of Lou so acutely I nearly lost it and I shuffled the cards and laid out a 7 spread with hands that just didn't shake and the camera swooped as I turned aces and told only good news. 'Ruby Red' to finish and the audience right there with me, made it a moment in other circumstances I would have enjoyed.

I didn't wait for the wrap party and local press, and slipped away on the next train to London. Once in the carriage the panic that had been suppressed all those hours crawled in my stomach, my legs, made me tremble uncontrollably. Did I meet the murdered Italian? What did I actually remember? Anything? There had been a party with Sinatra and other stars looking always smaller than one imagined. And exceptionally bright spotlights, an orchestra, the pool so brilliantly blue it was almost unreal. Was it in Rome? I couldn't remember anything about it. A palace? A red door? A pool so blue it drew me down into its depths, swirling, dizzy, a lethal pool. Was I remembering this because she'd told me this? There was something hypnotic about her. Her voice a touch rough but also soft and sometimes nice. No accent giving away where she came from, perhaps a suggestion of Chicago. For a while, at the beginning, I had taken whatever a party offered but not on a daily basis, not to blackout. The career came first. I certainly liked the freedom the substances gave me for a while, the shortest while. I didn't sleep around. I wanted love not experiment.

I'd tried phoning Kit most of the day and finally got her as I was coming into London. She told me to first check my flat for any message or possible visit and then take a taxi to the boudoir. Quickly I asked if she remembered a murder in Rome nineteen years ago.

'Which one of the thousand we know about?'

I had no idea what this woman, called Lou, would stage for my card reading debut at a Park Lane hotel. Why couldn't I get her off my back by doing one session for this man she wanted to fleece? That was the word. The sheep's coat. Did my guide have a sense of humour? It would never be just once. Because it was bigger and more corrupt than I could possibly know. She had never said anything about the number of times I'd be required to fit an Ace of Spades into the core directions she wanted the man to follow. I'd be hooked whatever it was.

As I crossed Paddington Station to the taxi rank I knew I had never known the Stephano victim. She'd described a wild and fatal evening and placed me at the telling moment. I wanted proof. I opened the front door without incident and climbed the stairs to the first floor and saw a semicircle of tarot cards outside the entrance to my flat. A King of Spades surrounded by seven negative and violent Major Arcana cards. What did it look like? A death threat? A murder? I thought immediately of the man in Rome. I didn't want to touch the cards and picked them up in order with a gloved hand as though they were poison.

I placed them in quarantine outside the window. Downstairs I checked the front door but there was no sign how Lou had got in. Using a plastic card? Ringing the bell of a neighbour upstairs? I tried but the woman didn't answer. I scribbled a message for Ray to call me, drank water, left the flat, went back and prayed for guidance. I took the cards off the window ledge and put them in a plastic bag to give to Kit. Then the phone rang. Expecting Lou, I lifted the receiver, but didn't speak. Howard told me how great I had been, the song superb, my performance uplifting. I was a star. I got out of the door before the next call and could hear it ringing as I sped down the stairs.

CHAPTER 18

'"THE SERAPHIM'S STRATAGEM".' Elmore looked along the spread of cards. 'Not well aspected.'

'What does it mean?'

He was more involved with the layout of the cards. 'They can be read from right to left or otherwise. The outcome is the same. Whoever laid this by your door knows their stuff. It's hardly a welcome mat.'

'Meaning?'

'The only way out is to lay a spread from the old times and so neutralise the effect.' He took a pack of ordinary playing cards and shuffled. 'It's called "Knowledge is Power".'

I pointed again to the tarot semicircle and asked who the King of Spades represented. At last I got an answer.

'He is a dark, ruthless, unscrupulous man sinking, who has interfered with the affairs of the heart of a fair woman, the Queen of Diamonds. Much sorrow.'

Fair. So it wasn't the woman called Lou on the train.

Elmore laid out 36 cards in rows of six and worried about the time I again asked when Kit was going to join us. He pointed to the first card. 'When covered with a heart, good luck will attend the hopes and plans of the enquirer.' He laid a card face down on top of the first card. 'If covered by a club, moderate good luck. If it's a diamond, evil rather than good influence. A spade means bad luck, robbery, financial ruin, disaster, possibly death.' He told me turn face up the covering card. I knew before I did so it would be a spade. He raised up his hands. 'Then we have to appeal to the fates.'

In his rich sonorous voice he recited incantations and made a tube of his hands and blew until the cards fluttered. He said it got rid of all bad energy. I still wanted to know what was 'The Seraphim's Stratagem'.

'A spider in the centre of its web. It waits to draw in the prey.'

'Is it a person?'

'A practice. She has shown by the layout of the eight cards she isn't just a player in the practice but something more lethal.'

'Which is?'

'An initiate.'

He collected the playing cards into a pile and I asked what was taking Kit so long.

'She's been called by a client to do a reading.' He looked at his watch. 'It must be a 90-minute booking. Or another client has also turned up.'

Believing I was short of time, I asked where the first client lived.

'Oh no. Kit's at the Jack of Clubs in Soho.'

I asked where exactly.

'A small alleyway off Meard Street. She goes there most days. It's there she makes her real money.'

*

The Jack of Clubs, a drinking joint, popular after the Second World War, had somehow, perhaps due to lack of money and fresh clientele, kept its original identity. The alley was poorly lit and the doorway to the courtyard not immediately visible. Its wood was cracked, its paint long past any actual colour, and it opened without objection onto the curiously untouched courtyard with its solitary gloomy lamp. The ease of entering made me pause. I'd have preferred some sort of normal security, a buzzer, a bell, a bouncer. The courtyard, long forgotten, held me back in the shadow and I could be in any time. And then from the building opposite came the unmistakable sound of live piano music and the ballad 'Smoke Gets in Your Eyes' from the fifties. The original club sign faded against the wall was just noticeable, and underneath a more recent qualification: 'Members Only'. This door too opened without formality and I climbed to the first floor of the unmodernised house, its wallpaper from my grandmother's time, torn in places revealing an even older design from the twenties or earlier. The stairs steep and somehow private with carpet worn and singed over the years by cigarettes, and the stale air rank with the ghosts of a thousand 'gin and its' and lavishly applied Coty perfume, popular forty years ago, and Player's fags. Another door opened easily into a room crowded and cheerful. Too many smoothly opening doors didn't feel right in my predicament. They fitted the awesome appearance that morning of the woman in the train carriage who logically could not be there. Was I now followed? Was she here?

The sofas in semi-collapse around the walls were claimed by regulars talking of old times. Behind the bar a black and white photograph of Montgomery Clift and adverts for beer. Nothing much had changed in here and that's how they liked it. The pianist lifted the tempo and couples got up and danced the mambo. The next song from South Pacific had everyone singing and the atmosphere was suddenly electric. Through an open door I could see an inner room and Kit, splendidly placed, reading cards. At the bar, various clairvoyant clients waited hopefully. 'Watch the drink,' advised the barman. 'She won't read for you if you've had one too many.' He'd worked there since the fifties and said he'd be happy to die on the premises. 'There's nowhere like this. Doesn't exist.' And he pointed through to where Kit sat beside a lamp. 'Got up to the nines. Who does that anymore?'

131

Along the walls a careless arrangement of photos, witness to a time when the club had its heyday, Jean Simmons, Stewart Grainger, Ann Sheridan, Patricia Roc, Margaret Lockwood, James Mason. My interest pleased the barman. The fifties music world was well represented. The Ink Spots, Frankie Laine, Jonny Ray, The Searchers. I asked if they always had card readings.

'Monday nights, the First Coven of White Witches still have their moot upstairs.' He straightened a picture of Vincent Price. 'You'd be surprised the ones that still come here.'

And then I saw the snapshot. It made me sit down on the nearest seat. It was of the guru Shanti Opal. I didn't need to look again. I'd seen her in the newspapers a mere month ago. I asked the barman who she was and he shuffled around to examine the wall. The snapshot was stuck on casually with Bluetack. Other more famous photographs took the attention.

'Can't say I know her.'

'Has she been here?'

'Maybe she's one of the showgirls from the clubs. They still come in for a chat and a drink.'

I didn't tell him she was a reincarnated divinity.

In the other room Kit's client paid cash and got up rosy with life belief and the prospect of tall, dark and handsome. The next in line was already at the doorway, but Kit waved to me and for a moment I did hesitate. I remembered the far from dulcet tones assuring Starlight she wasn't left behind, the way she spoke about a new reader's inevitable lack of free will when it came to the racket. It didn't fit with the graceful seer. 'They get caught in the racket same as everyone else. Tarnished, they want to milk the system for all they can get.' She had her rough side.

It was 8.50 and I sped through a summary of the encounter as I lay out the eight tarot cards in order in front of her.

'Is it a curse?'

She wasn't as impressed as Elmore. 'Only if you want it to be.' Her eyes were steady and not as friendly as before. I realised of course she'd had a job to do, get me on the psychic circuit and that was achieved. Sadie Chill was happy. What else was there to do with me apart from remembering the showtime, in both our cases over? I asked what the tarot spread meant.

'A man through bad aspects is sinking. It could be a prediction rather than a fulfilment.' She looked at her watch without bothering to hide her impatience. 'There are five waiting out there and I'm running late.'

'But what am I to do?' Not quite desperate but getting there.

'Match her. See what her play is and up the stakes.'

'It's not a poker game.'

'It might be.' She spoke automatically.

'And the guru's photo is out there.' I insisted she come and see it. She did not move.

'She gestured to the barman and asked for a mineral water. 'Keep hold of the punters. Offer them something on the house.' To me she said, 'That's it, Toots. After all I didn't put her in your backyard.'

Yes, she had her rough side.

✳

10.30 – and I almost reached for the phone, expecting a call. For the last six months my life had been full of Mrs Longbridge, Vinnie, Rosanne, and they and their like had become a habit not easy to break. I had to remind myself I was not logged on. The lights came up, bright in the pub, and I went to the window half expecting to see something meaningful in the street. Lou in an Aston Martin, Lou looking up at my windows, Lou in the company of muscled men who got what she wanted. I ran a bath and in the mirror did the daily voice exercises. When the phone rang I almost answered in the usual way. Welcome. My name's Isis.

She allowed a pause as I knew she would. Did I have an answer ready? She was waiting at some West End hotel and in one of the rooms a man had arrived to see what destiny was offered. Starlight laughed. 'Forgotten the introduction already? You'll be busy with bigger things. Sadie has signed a deal with a European company. They're coming into the business. Big bucks. Everything will change except the readers' wages. Internet, website, tours, TV, everything. You'll never stop. Don't let on you know.'

I was going to ask her about other matters but, excited, she'd hung up, eager to pass on the bombshell to other paupers down the line.

Lou with the slightly slanted hazel green eyes, black chignon, a little wild, the perfect mouth, was maybe accompanying a man in a Park Lane hotel, waiting at an airport, even outside my flat. Wherever it was she kept it to herself and eleven o'clock came and ticked on towards twelve. She did not ring and I'd so much have preferred it if she had.

✳

'What was the date exactly?' Ray wrote 1980.

'Eighteen years ago. I told you. It was one of my first gigs. I was twenty-one.

'So "Ruby Red" was much later. Ten years at least.' He wrote more figures and I saw he included my actual age, thirty-eight, from which I'd lopped off two years since meeting him. I asked what difference 'Ruby Red' made.

'It did well in Italy and Ricco Stephano had been at least ten years dead. There was no connecting you with his killing. And there would have been. Someone would have come to you for money. Or they'd have threatened to go to the press. It would have made quite a story. Or his family would have taken some revenge. What do you remember about the Stephano party?'

He'd spent the day doing a police and press search of the killing in Rome and I tried to be helpful. I thought I might have been there because I remembered the bright blue of the pool and the established singers and stars. Had I met Sinatra? I'd remember that.

He wanted more. I could not remember more. He asked what I'd drunk in those days.

'As it came.'

Where did I go the next day? It was a long time ago, a time when I could do two parties a night. It wasn't something I ever thought about, not part of my life. If someone had been murdered and I was there I'd have been questioned. I'd remember that. He asked what I did remember about that time in a tone that suggested it had all been obliterated by drink and drugs.

'I did the Italian songs in those days. Oh, yes, they called me the waif. I was skinny and blonde and looked too young.

He shuffled through photocopies of newspaper reports. 'It sounds like a very small party. No mention of who was there.'

'Does it say how he died?'

'Shot by an unknown assailant.'

'And her?'

'No mention of a model from the Ford agency USA here. They played it down. I'm not good at Italian but I got the waiter opposite to run it through for me. In some papers it seems the occasion was hardly bigger than a dinner party for the family. Certainly no celebrities. No Sinatra. What a let-down. I feel sorry for the guy. But your agent at that time – yes, he's still around – remembers differently.' He waited for me to be surprised. 'You do remember Al?' He turned so he could see my reaction. 'Don't you?'

Of course I hadn't forgotten, but would I like what Al remembered? 'What did he say?'

He turned back to the handwritten notes and said I was in Rome on a try-out and on the night Ricco was shot I had performed in three different venues.

'What did Al say?'

'He doesn't. He didn't go on to the party, but you could have been taken there. The next day you went back to the UK for a booking at Ronnie Scott's.

I remembered that. 'A try-out.'

Ray had more questions to which I had no answers. He went to the Italian embassy, spent hours on the phone. His conclusion let me remain innocent.

'If anyone had anything on you they'd have come to light with "Ruby Red". You were substantial in those days.'

And then I got the answer. 'She was the only witness. She's kept it on ice for a rainy day. She thinks she can put me beside the corpse. Photographs? What does she have?'

He did the wide open hands gesture which he used a lot these days. 'What does it matter what she has? We can't find her.'

And then it occurred to me that maybe we should. Give her something to worry about for a change. Five days till the next gig.

We spent the afternoon looking through glossy magazines from eighteen years ago. Ray even got the agency lists. There was just one. The eyes very still could be Lou's eyes but they weren't slanted. And they were blue. But the expression, still and deep, was like hers. The mouth gave nothing away. In each shot she smiled or pouted.

'She was just beginning,' he said. 'Looked the business. They called her "La Divina", "the divine one".'

He spent the rest of the day on the young model, born in Brooklyn, liked the outdoors, loved horses, was best pals with her Mom. The agency had secured her a good contract, but like a lot of people in this story she just dropped out.

Although he admitted her PR description was horse shit, there was no point going further. How did you find 'La Divina'? And she did not resemble the woman on the train.

*

I wished she would ring and get it over with. Where was the 'husband' who needed redemption? Even the 'brother' who needed directions. How could I be so deeply in this that they needed blackmail to get me shuffling cards? They were prepared to try and threaten my very existence. I could still see Lou's face reflected on and on in the train window, lit by sunlight with shadow cutting through like prison bars. I should start my tour of the north of England the following month, but my agent thought I'd do better with the psychic kind. Who's side was he on? Obviously not mine. The bank manager's? He said he'd got a good idea. 'Let's blend the two shows, psychic and singing. Use the new songs. I'll talk to the company.'

'Sadie Chill?'

'Better than that. She's selling out to a European entertainment company. Telephone psychic is becoming big business. They'll pay for the rights of you using your new material. It's almost clairvoyant the way it's happened.'

I wish I thought so. I asked for the booking figures so far for me on my own tour. I didn't need to be psychic to see 'blend' was the way to go. His parting shot: 'Clairvoyance? It's nothing to be ashamed of,' could have killed my day.

I did the psychic photo-shoot and press release with Howard in a Camden studio and several company members present. I asked for Sadie Chill, expecting to see her, and was told she was busy with the company deal. I asked what she looked like, just to be sure. These days I needed to know about the absent ones. She was fat, so she was out. Howard seemed to be in charge, but obviously had no experience, so the photographer took over and suggested we build the PR around 'Ruby Red' and I wear a flame-coloured wig. The hair must be plenteous and spread wild around my face. Twice his assistant called from the wig maker to check some detail. The third time Howard, irritated, suggested I speak directly and give the assistant my head measurements. There was too much noise in the studio and I could not hear the caller. I said to phone back and was about to replace the receiver.

'Baa, baa, black sheep, have you any wool? You'd better have.'

It was the most menacing she'd sounded even with the disturbance around me. I shouted to the group for silence.

'Tell him you see his grandmother. You're good on those,'

and I listened to what I'd heard before. 'He'll call you.' Her voice was surely hypnotic. 'This is how you'll play it. Just as I tell you. He will call you.' Hypnotic over. 'Get a pen and paper and start writing.'

So the hotel was out. The guy had not arrived or not agreed to the reading. Why did I think things weren't exactly going her way? We were back with the older, cheaper method.

'His nickname's Mischa. Call him that and surprise him. Your guide is good on nicknames. Here's what you do. Ask for ten per cent up front and the rest as usual. He'll understand. And remember, Isis – or is it Jesse? – that "Ruby Red" is not everyone's favourite.'

I was going to confront her and demand a meeting, but the sound of her voice again took over and I listened as though in an altered state and found I could not speak.

✳

The brother phoned first and made sure I was agreeable, that I knew my lines, not that 'ten per cent up front and the rest as usual' were hard to remember.

'And give a thought to the Ricco affair.'

I decided not to answer.

He didn't allow time to pass. 'You're thinking it's a while ago but you're still sitting pretty for it.'

I thought it wise still not to answer. He hung up.

The husband seemed well-mannered like the first time he'd called. He also sounded tired. This was a call he did not choose to make. I started to give him the lines in the way Lou requested, but he cut through before I got to the money.

'Who are you?'

What should I say? No spirit guides to help me. Just silence. I said, 'Who are you?'

Ray wrote quickly on the back of Lou's instruction sheet. 'Get his number.'

'Are you a medium? Is there such a thing as a guide? Please tell me.'

He sounded gentle and didn't belong in this story at all. Nothing I could discern linked him with Lou or the brother. He didn't like my delay.

As though risking being overheard I spoke more softly. 'Do nothing. No action.'

Ray stabbed a finger on the paper repeatedly. 'Phone number. Get it.'

'So what do I do?' the man asked.

'Pray. Ask for protection.'

'So I need it.'

Definitely. This man needed the best there was.

'What are you? I see money all around you.' Not quite right but I needed to keep him on the line. It had to be about money.

'I'm a banker.'

'Give me your phone number, Mischa, and your location.'

He paused. 'You must be psychic to call me that.'

'I am told your fear will pass. The guide promises that.'

I'd taken a blind shot but what else would have put this kind of man on a telephone psychic line.

'Give me your number and the situation will be dealt with.' Who was I talking to? Mrs 'In the Box?' Rosanne? A bored housewife?

I could hear him sigh then decidedly he gave a mobile number and an address in Lausanne. I supposed he didn't think he had much to lose.

'Do something,' he said, not without a noticeable desperation. Then he hung up. I wasn't wrong about the fear.

Ray and I spoke at the same time. If he was bugged that would be that. She'd get to him.

Ray took his passport, checked his credit cards. 'Just in case of bug I'll call him from the street. I'll fly out and see him.'

I asked him what he thought I should do.

'It's obvious they haven't got him, otherwise they wouldn't have to use you. Maybe he will buy into your fluff and give her

139

what she wants. She must have tried more obvious ways. If he calls again wise him up discreetly, so he pulls out.'

'All that glitters is not gold. Is that it?'

'You flop but who can blame you. She knows fortune-telling was never your thing.'

'Police?'

'They'll never believe you.'

'Sadie?'

'I don't think she'll see it as her problem.'

✷

I wouldn't sleep and did what so many insomniacs were driven to do. I became a caller. I wanted Grey Owl but got a girl with a boy's broken voice. Like most she was good, bad. There was an E around me. Everyone had an E.

'She's very attractive and someone who will always get her own way.'

That fitted less people. 'Can you describe her?'

'Thinking of her stirs up the spirits.'

That didn't sound too good. What else?

She said I had it rough but everything was going to get better. I'd even meet tall, dark and handsome.

I did what so many had done to me. I hung up. I tried Kit but got Elmore and wanted to estimate how dangerous my situation might become.

'The Seraphim's Stratagem. What does it mean if laid out by an initiate?'

'It becomes more powerful. It's a gateway into other realities. In bad hands it's a trap.'

'How do you become an initiate?'

'Through ritual and practice to gain attunement. You need certain practices that are given secretly. It's handed on from one initiate to another.'

'Do you have to be spiritual?' I was sure that left Lou out.

140

'It's not a moral issue.' Again he was kind and said he would place protection around me using ritual from ancient Egypt.

'How can they accuse me of being present at a crime scene where I had not even set foot. The lack of blackmail calls when "Ruby Red" came out proved that.'

'Set foot.' And I could for a moment see a delicate foot in a high-heeled shoe step into a dark puddle, and the pale tulle skirt, long to the ankles flick its ends disdainfully through the liquid and turn the colour of dark rust. The step was uncaring and drops splashed up the side of the skirt and stayed.

'Is she mesmerising me, Elmore?' I did not want to let him go. Could a person pass on thoughts to another so they became theirs? What else is clairvoyance?

'She obviously needs you to set up the money source which has gone cold. Your voice is unique. He's heard it. She can't change now, she obviously represented you as a phenomenal seer.'

'I'm no clairvoyant.'

He coughed politely. 'Don't advertise it. The woman has found out where you're weak so she can pressurise you. What do you remember?'

'My head is so full of other people's lives I can hardly remember the night before leave alone eighteen years ago. I was not at a murder scene. I just see the pale skirt, its ends trailing in blood. I can hear the flick of the material in the liquid.'

'You were a young girl and wanted to be part of life, to dance your dance, to live to be high.'

'It's a lot better than low.'

'You'll come up again,' he promised and sounded kind. And then Kit took the phone.

'It's after hours. Where's the fire?'

I tried to tell her about Lou's calls.

'But she's done nothing, so what are you worried about? Get some sleep. You've got Manchester in two days.'

And then I remembered the guru speaking Lou's lines: 'I love you, Isis'. 'She uses her. And the guru's snapshot is in the club.

141

Someone put it there.'

'Well, of course. It didn't fly through the window.'

'It's the one in the evening paper. But a snapshot. So someone who knew her took it.'

Kit sighed. 'Even the regulars in that place stray off to see a phenomenon.'

'How can I find her? The Guru.'

'Call her up. Make a psychic connection. Light a candle and see her face in your mind and, concentrating on that, say "Come to me now." Say it twenty-five times then blow out the candle. Relight it the next night, same thing – five nights in all. Goodnight.' She hung up.

There was something wrong with that club, more a house along a forgotten alley of London. In an area where land was so highly sought after and priced, how could such a site remain untouched? It wasn't the stuff of today but belonged in memory.

*

I worked for the psychic line. I'd better use it. I didn't know who to trust. Starlight? Betty? Sadie Chill? I asked for Jade. At first it was no, she was booked for weeks, and then the booking guy smartened up and remembered they needed me in Manchester.

'You sure this is an emergency reading, Isis? I can't do this every day.' He put me through.

Jade spoke automatically without pause. 'They are trying to use you because you've been well known and that will impress the – they call him "the mark". You're good cover, can go anywhere. They'll say if you do one last thing they'll leave you alone, but they won't. They'll try and frighten you, then offer inducements.'

'So what do I do?' I was already frightened.

Jade paused. 'The "mark", I'm told, is the way out, because he still doesn't quite know what they're up to. Never forget you're a winner and meant to perform. Leave when they least expect it.'

'They? Give me the "they".'

'It's all about her. Understand her and you'll know them.'
And, kindly, she said goodbye and hung up.
Understand her? How?

✳

Ray didn't ring until late morning and said not to take any
calls. He was leaving from Geneva airport and when he needed
contact he'd phone my mobile. Before I could ask anything he'd
hung up. Although I'd been up for hours and seemed to be wide
awake, I lay on the bed and sank quickly into an image-filled
half sleep that I couldn't resist, that I couldn't lift up from and,
overflowing with memories, I was undoubtedly moving towards
a red door slightly open in a crumbling wall. I pushed through
into a darkly lit entrance that housed the famous, all that I
wanted to be. Again I saw the pale tulle skirt and the fresh blood
splashed along the layered hem. I slept wishing to be well out of
it. Automatically I picked up the ringing phone, ready with the
Isis introduction.

'Hey, hey, Jesse. Not so good.' She sounded hostile. 'You're
going to have to do better. Get your thoughts out of the sheep
trough and bleat in his ear loud and good. Certain people from
Rome want to catch up with you and it's not for an autograph.
Like I said, "Ruby Red" is not everyone's favourite song.'

I wished I had a response that would shock her. 'I remember
your tulle skirt . . .'

She didn't even hesitate. 'You were off your face. What can
you remember? The body blocking the door? And you couldn't
get it open? Couldn't get out? You keep thinking did I meet Ricco.
Well, if that isn't meeting the dude tell me what is. You're asking
the wrong question. Change it to what gets me out of this.'

'If you ever get short of money they'd love you on line.' I was
sick of being frightened.

'Just think, end of the line for Isis. He will call you again.
Just say the lines and keep counting sheep.'

Click of disconnection. I should have remembered Ray's instruction. Trying to challenge her was not smart. Had she been aware of my call from Mischa. I didn't think so. I felt she was still – unusually for her – powerless. And power was what she lived on. Was Mischa the sinking man in the 'Seraphim's Stratagem'. A high initiate had left those tarot cards spelling out a message. Lou? I was getting used to voices and hers changed slightly with each call. She was not anymore full of red coins and red aces, the high money of late winter. Could she hypnotise me from a distance and cause those intrusive images? Or was it just my exhaustion from months of struggle in a world I did not understand.

Ray asked me to join him in a rehearsal room in Soho and be anonymous, so I supposed he too was using strategy. I was prepared for catastrophe prognosis, something life-changing and yet he had little to say and talked about the flight. He looked as he would say: 'wired', and sighed, obviously exhausted. Had he been up all night drinking with the banker? He looked around as though checking the seemingly empty rehearsal room. Suspicious? On edge? More small talk. It was the last thing I expected. If it wasn't for the 7 of Diamonds in the 'Is he faithful spread?', I'd have said he'd been out on the lash with a Swiss tart instead of saving my life.

'What about the banker Ray. Get your mind on it.'

'Von Elman is not a banker. He owns the bank. Several banks. He's from the Middle East and has more than one name.' Ray spoke quickly, his voice low. 'He says from your description this woman Lou is a model.'

'What do you mean, my description?'

'He didn't immediately agree he knew her, so I described her as best I could.'

'Hasn't he met her?'

'At first I wasn't sure but later in the game he did admit there was a model who had her hooks into him.'

'Is he crooked?'

'I didn't think so. I'd say he was an ethical person, very professional.'

'So how has she got him?'

'Could be he's married and . . .'

'But he didn't seem to recognise her. What does he say about her?'

'Not a lot.'

'But, Ray, he's frightened. Did he not admit that?'

'With me he was cautious.' Another big sigh.

I waited for more, expected more, but the subject seemed to have come to an end.

'Ray, does he know who I am?'

'Yes. There seemed no point not telling him. He hasn't made up his mind if he believes in all that spirit guidance, but I made it up for him. I said it's crap. He's sorry you're going through all this. He's considerate. I went through the Rome business and he understands you're being used. That's when he thought he knew who you're talking about. Your best out is the following. When she next calls, say "Rinaldo from Jimmy's Bar in Rome says hello." That will close her down.'

He looked at his watch again and decided he should do the Festival Hall concert that night.

'I think this woman Lou was obviously a sexual indiscretion. What Lou wants Lou gets. She doesn't like cut-off and he has definitely cut off.'

'Her name can't be Lou.'

'Eva Calvo Ludici. He says she was present among the famous at the Stephano party. She was seventeen and going places. The Ford Agency, after the murder, dropped her. They were afraid of a scandal and it broke her career. It seems he helped her. He didn't specify how.'

'Did he have something to do with it? The Stephano business?'

'He said the killing was political. The police raked it over but there were no witnesses. By the time the police did come everybody had left.'

'Who was Stephano?'

'A businessman. Wanted in in politics. Got too much power. It was a Mafia killing. Case closed. Only Stephano's supporters never believed it.'

'How did he know all this?'

'He didn't say. I think there's a lot he didn't say'

'Did she do it?'

'He was uneasy talking about her. Maybe he is frightened. Back then in 1980 he rescued her and closed down her past. So just say the lines he suggested.'

I was doing a lot of that these days. I didn't believe it was the whole story. Did Ray? More silence, unusual for him.

'What will she do to me?'

'Just get her off your back.' He stood up and said until the business was over he'd ring me before coming to the flat. I'd never seen him so evasive. He'd been gone all night and most of the morning supposedly in the company of a man who owned a bank, but according to this account had no more than an hour's worth of conversation. What did they do the rest of the time? Had the banker taken him out for a night with other Eva Calvo Ludici's. Had he been out on his own with less grand girls of the night?

'So will this banker call me? Will he give her what she wants? Or will he shut her up? Come on, Ray. What went on?'

'He doesn't say much,' Ray decided.

I thought he wasn't the only one.

CHAPTER 19

'RINALDO FROM JIMMY'S BAR in Rome says hello.' It wasn't enough. What was Lou really about? Who could I ask? Ray seemed off the air, aloof as though stunned. Having to ring in code before coming to my flat didn't sound too good. The banker who seemed to be the problem may or may not deal with Lou. I tried to call him but the mobile was switched off. Who actually knew this woman Eva Calvo Ludici? Possibly the guru with the interposed message. Could it have been jumbled words or just coincidence? How could I find her? Finally I decided I'd better take care of myself.

There had to be some surer way of making it safe. Perhaps I should use what I did to be free of them. Up the ante as Kit had advised. And then I got it – the way out. I asked Howard for recordings of my calls with Lou, the man called Mischa, the brother. He said this meant going back through months of files and was reluctant. I explained I needed to get rid of a possible blackmail problem which would certainly affect Sadie's exciting sale to Europe. That had Howard biking the tapes to me within the hour. He did ask why I hadn't involved Sadie. I said I didn't want to worry her when she had so much on. I realised I still had never seen her. Why? Just a thought. Was she really fat? What did she look like? Howard described someone who could never be the woman reflected endlessly on the train.

Lou called, as I knew she would, during the twilight time, the blue hour as the French called it.

'You're cooked, Isis. I can't do anything about it. You're free, white and at least twenty-one as they used to say.'

'You got me in it.'

'Prove it.' She laughed, and I could almost see the jagged teeth.

Had he given her money? Lou could probably get past 'cut off'. But it didn't sound as though she liked me.

'I have a message for you from spirit.' I started the tape rolling with her early list of psychic messages for the husband.

'You can't use it. Private material. Not admissible.' She sounded confident.

'A copy sits where it'll be useful if anything unwise should occur. My guide indicates it won't.' I started the second tape. 'My guide says I'm looked after.' I let her hear the banker's voice, just a touch. It didn't worry her. I lowered the volume. 'And I get a Rinaldo from Jimmy's Bar in Rome. He says hello. Hey, he calls you Eva.'

Shocked, silent. It was like killing a dangerous insect.

'But he's dead.' Her voice was deader.

'Of course. So I'm not the dumb reader I used to be.'

She didn't put down the receiver as fast as she used to. I didn't think she'd cut off at all. Although my receiver was properly replaced, I felt there was some link activated between my presence in the room and her thoughts wherever they came from. The silence continued through the blue hour and then I seemed to hear the sound of phones ringing and snatches of conversations running one into another in this night world where truth was as hard to find as the spirit guides on a celestial trail through the heavens.

*

The psychic shows could have gone on indefinitely and by the sixth month on Sky TV I could shuffle cards while climbing scarlet stairs to sing 'Ruby Red'. Astrological signs spun around my bush fire red hair and tarot cards rose from my heart chakra bringing luck to audience members holding identical ones.

A year on the road and I had a prediction column in a tabloid and contract offer to tour Australia. Someone had told me to get out when 'they' least expected it. There was no more 'they'. I hadn't heard from Lou again so it wasn't that angle. More likely my career needed another direction if it was going to survive. Some of my fans from the old days thought I was dead. The Himalayan debt mountain was more a hill but I couldn't go on with this mindless entertainment which took me further from my true path than I could afford to admit. It was worse than being a phone psychic. I almost called Kit to see if anything good was on the horizon, but did I really believe it? My hands full of aces in front of TV cameras while giving love, money, and chance to the audience, signing psychic advice letters written by Howard to my growing mass of fans had killed off any slight belief I might have had in another realm. I'd be mad to believe any of it. Like the guru business, clairvoyance had saturated the public and the tidal wave was now on its way out.

Ray was running his own band and touring Europe and occasionally I did wonder who he'd met on that urgent visit to Lausanne. He was never quite the same afterwards but I couldn't pinpoint the change and he didn't want any confrontation on that subject. If I was clairvoyant I'd say he'd met someone.

The escape came in a way I couldn't have foreseen and doubted Jade or any of the others would either. The Victorian music hall by the Thames went dark through lack of money and Ray suggested we take it on. I'd always liked music hall but it had never occurred to me I'd do it. Here it was unchanged from the turn of the century and I still had the voice, loved the nostalgia, but where was the backing?

'Oh, come on,' said Ray, 'you're not afraid of a debt. The theatre seats 900 and we'll get the tourists.' People in the business joined us and as a group of forty we took it on. And now I was free, freed from the ace of spades, the 'Seraphim's Stratagem', and the Ruby Red good news shows. It was becoming the best time.

I met Ray's friend from the orchestra whom I'd last seen outside the Shanti Opal event at the Albert Hall. He asked if I'd heard anything about her. 'She seems to have gone to ground. A lot of her followers expected she'd tour South America.' He remembered the 'I love you, Isis' inclusion during her London appearance and put it down to coincidence. I almost agreed. 'It's over now, the guru business. Come and gone,' he concluded.

I described the model Lou to see if she'd been around the venues. What about Eva Calvo Leducci? He didn't remember.

'Oh, you'd remember Lou.' And it brought back for a moment the unanswered questions. Where was she? Had she on the train hypnotised me so I received images of events that had nothing to do with me. In her company I had felt a shift, a change most unwelcome. Was she the Stephano killer? The best person to ask was Elmore and he was pleased to hear from me.

'We watch your shows. Of course it's just a job, but even we light workers have to make a living. You are still a star. You'll never lose that quality.'

I thanked him and got on to the real subject: who and what was Lou?

'Don't dwell on bad things. You only give them energy.'

'It all seems so inconclusive.'

'But you're out of all that now. Of course the company will look after you. Kit told you that.'

What about the small theatre company? Would music hall do it? I told him about the new development, how we were rehearsing, how it was authentic music hall, and would be up and going before Christmas.

He thought it was wonderful and offered some of the songs he'd collected. 'Don't even think about the other matter. She was just a working girl trying it on. Nothing special.'

The problem was she was special. I'd seen her. And the Jack of Clubs oddly intriguing was also special. I almost went there on one occasion just to see if it really existed. And then the music hall took off and I left behind the hard months with their murky mystery. Instead of 'Ruby Red' I sang 'Underneath the Arches'.

I did see Kit on the Kentish Town Road late on a winter's afternoon, food-shopping. There wasn't much to say. The psychic line, now the European company had taken over, was too slick and no fun. I told her about the music hall wanting but not daring to know if it would last.

'But I told you you'd sing the old songs.'

And I remembered my first visit two summers before to the Kentish Town house. She had predicted 'old' and 'nostalgia'. No more to say it seemed, so I did quite unnecessarily ask about the 'Seraphim's Stratagem'. Was it real? Did it exert influence?

'So I'm told.'

'Well it's over for me.'

'When it's over,' – she paused – 'the "Seraphim's Stratagem" has to work itself out.'

We said goodbye and she went into the supermarket and I to the theatre.

CHAPTER 20

NOVEMBER, AND WE WERE four weeks in and still running.
By spring the box office takings should break even, and I walked
across Primrose Hill daring to feel as I used to – good in myself.

Up the stairs to the flat, unlock the door and inside something
was wrong. It was the light. From the window a shaft of bright
sunlight and yet it was a grey winter's day. Cautious now, I
walked softly and left the door ajar, just in case. No one there.
Not too easily persuaded I checked the other rooms. Just the
sunlight, one shaft, and as I watched I could see bars of darkness
cutting through like prison bars and the more I stared the more
I discerned a figure between the bars as though crouched in a
cell. She had long blonde hair, blue eyes, a composed lovely face.
I could see teeth so I supposed she was smiling. I hoped that
was it. And this figure was reflected on and on without limit
in the beam of light. I heard a sound, then another. It wasn't
exactly a voice. I thought it said, 'Isis'. And I started moving
backwards, too scared to make one sound in this place where I
no longer belonged. Don't draw attention. Even breathing had
to be silent. When I judged the distance to be safe I turned and
would have run from the flat, but a small rolling noise stopped
all flight, a hard noise like a marble moving across a wooden

floor, a noise that could not be there and I looked back and at the bottom of the cage of light a marble was rolling quite indifferent, set on its course. A dark blue and yellow glass with a pale blue circle and as it came nearer I saw it wasn't a marble but the rolling eyeball of my dream. The yellow light pinged out like a fused lamp leaving the room as expected, a sullen grey.

I stayed standing, no point sitting in these circumstances, and checked myself for unwelcome reactions. I felt surprisingly all right as though the light was actually inside me soothing like honey. But I felt there was an edge and beyond that it was not all right and that's where the eyeball rolled. I had no explanation for what I had seen and got myself to Kit's place.

She met me in the boudoir where she was preparing herself for an evening of ritual with other clairvoyants and mystics.

'November 8th is the original Celtic New Year.' She wore a silver cross in which each line was equal so it formed a square. Her make-up was white paste until she patted on the foundation cream. Age had come suddenly to this lovely face and there was not a lot even a surgeon could do. It was an inside job. She listened to the story impatiently and I changed 'cage' to 'cell', and the figure was not imprisoned but waiting. It reminded me of something I'd heard. 'The Seraphim's Stratagem' – I asked her what it was and why.

'A manifestation.' She spoke calmly. 'It is the Celtic New Year when spirits come through to us and we advance towards them. So not surprising that today the projection of the Seraphim's Stratagem could manifest so strongly in your room.'

'But it was waiting for me. It was like another reality in mine.'

'Exactly.'

'It wasn't her, Lou. This figure was blonde, blue-eyed and her teeth were even and good. She was shorter.' I realised that now. 'Why has this happened?'

'Just a reminder.' She powdered her face and a few years lifted. 'That the initiate still has the power.'

'But she's not there. How can she produce that effect in my room.'

'By attunement. She, if it is a she, has power to direct that relentless, reflecting prison into your environment.'

'Why?'

'So you see it.' She turned over the 78 record of a French song. 'You see her. She's in that prison.'

'What does she want?'

Now Kit paused. 'To be taken notice of.'

She finished off the make-up and I asked if she could do my cards. Into the salon where the lamps were lit, and we sat at one of the small card tables while she shuffled the slim deck of large rectangular cards. The 10 of Swords kept coming up showing the female trapped inside a cell speared with knives, almost what I'd seen. She pulled out the card and waved it in front of me. 'This is an initiate with high powers of transformation that she achieves by hypnosis.'

'How?'

'She'll concentrate deeply on you and then visualise what she wants you to receive and then she sends it mind to mind. If you're unlucky you pick it up and it'll be etched in your thoughts. But it's not arisen from inside you. Remember that. It comes from outside from an imprint conveyed by her.'

'Mind games.'

'More an attuning and sending of the image.' Kit looked at the cards for some minutes. 'She's had an unlawful life. Think about her. What were your early impressions?'

Unlawful. I remembered her laughing about that. What had I said? I see a man with a sheep's hair. 'Maybe it's a wig, Isis. Maybe he's a judge, oh dear.' That's when she laughed. So I did see it.

'She has a hypnotic gift. Evil exists and is not sickness. Remember that.' She shuffled again and the layout showed brighter cards. No. 10 of Swords.

'She's gone over you with a tooth comb. Knows every date, every country, even what you wore. What you sang. Who the producers were. She knows where you're vulnerable. The red door in the crumbling wall. She could put you there. Were you there?'

155

'Not there.' I spoke too quickly.

'How can you remember? You were smoking and sniffing in those days.'

'Whatever.' I shrugged. 'I didn't kill anyone.'

'She must have a lot riding on the chance you did, to go to all that effort.'

Elmore drew close to the table and looked at the spread of cards. 'Ah, the King of Swords. We've seen him before. And the fair queen.' He picked up both cards and held them.

'"The King unseen lurked in her hand and mourned his captive queen".' He replaced the two cards. '"Soon as she spreads her cards the aerial guard descend and sit on each important card."' He turned to me. 'That's how it works, clairvoyance.'

'It's a past life business.' Kit folded the cards and wrapped them in a silk scarf. 'The Spanish say if you meet someone you think you have known in another life cross yourself, turn and walk away and behave as though you've seen a ghost.'

'But what can I do?' I looked from one to another. Was I any the wiser for the reading? I put two twenty pound notes on the table.

'Just go on with your life,' said Kit. She pointed to the door.

Not sensing she had any concern for my safety, I was suddenly furious. 'You're crazy. I'm not going out there.' I looked at the street.

She stood up, equally angry, and pushed the money back to me. 'You're in my home, still half broke, running from a crazed demon, too scared to leave. I can go out whenever I wish. Free. So tell me, who's the crazy one.'

*

I wondered what it was about the club that seemed off key. The snapshot made it part of my story. What really went on there? It was no more permanent than a stage set and had more in common with the cage of yellow light than everyday reality. I went back to prove it was real. I did not expect to find it or the guru's snapshot still on the wall or even the house itself across the courtyard. Had I simply stepped into another time?

Late afternoon and the atmosphere was ordinary as a supermarket. A few customers sat on stools around the bar, others played cards at the small tables. I went straight to the wall with photographs of the fifties movie stars and the snapshot was barely visible under a photograph of Jack Hawkins. The barman recognised me immediately as a client of Kit and gave me a tonic with lemon.

'So it's still here.' I pointed to the snapshot. 'Who could have put it up?'

He pulled it free from the wall and turned it over. It was blank.

'Is it the guru Shanti Opal?'

He said he didn't know, handed it to me and straightened up the other slightly slipping photos. A woman with long fair hair moved behind us to the bar and he left me to serve her.

'The barflies are quiet today,' she said. 'Let's give them all a proper drink.'

Corks popped and bottles fizzed and the woman proposed a toast. I stared at the snapshot, trying to make out the background. For a minute I thought it was this club. Her hair was pale gold, long, lustrous, the eyes light, their expression hard to define. Far seeing might describe it. The face was well boned and the beautiful lips were like those of the woman on the train but the teeth were even and clean. I asked the barman if the woman had been photographed by the bar. I pointed to the background.

'Could be. But a while ago. It's black and white. And taken with an old camera.'

Why didn't I see that? I asked if I could keep it and he saw no reason why not. I took it with me to the theatre.

✳

I didn't feel comfortable in my flat – the cage in sunlight had been too intrusive. If it was true that a psychic or initiate could send beams of light then it wasn't over. Why was I even part of this? What could I do? Go after her? I called Starlight, who was still on line for the same rates, and asked if she'd look at the snapshot. We met in a café in Primrose Hill and she said immediately the woman was Shanti Opal. 'She's finished. She'll have to reinvent herself.'

'Why?'

'There's no money anymore. Gurus are not big business anymore as once they were. But she was special. She was tops.'

'Did she make a lot of money?'

'It's not her so much. It's who's behind her.'

'What does that mean?'

'The ones who run her.'

I asked Starlight if she could find out where she was now. Could she try Sadie Chill who'd been such a fan?

'If you do an ad on the sex line. We need more business. Too many rivals out there.'

I walked away still looking at the snapshot. Why did I want all this? I wanted to meet her. No, I wanted to confront her. More – I wanted to defeat her. I did not want to be a victim.

✳

Ray unpacked his bag and asked for strong tea. He'd done sixty gigs, sometimes two a night at towns and cities across Europe and he said although they'd made money the band refused to work that way again. He'd found a solo violinist ideal for the music hall. He drank the tea as he pulled off his boots. It was then he picked up the snapshot forgotten on the table. It seemed everything else went out of his mind as he looked with consternation at this far-seeing guru who brought light to this world.

'How did you get it?' he said, finally.

I asked if he knew who she was.

'Do you?' He sounded as though he was making an effort to be neutral.

'The photo, or one like it, was in the tabloids.'

He still didn't answer so I tried another angle. 'Is it the guru?'
'I don't like the look of her. I don't want you to go near her.
Let's keep it simple. We're ahead of the game for once.' I noticed
he didn't let go of the snapshot and I crossed over to my well-
travelled dusty lover, kissed him and as the moment grew into
something else he relinquished the photo and I slipped it into
a half open drawer. On to the bed with him and he took away
further thought. He was worth waiting for.

✳

The voice was not Lou's and yet at first I thought it could have
been. It had a calm almost pleasing sound, one you'd want
to listen to and yet I was sure it had been worked on and the
elocution lessons and the diction practice had smoothed rough
edges. Yes the voice was at its best as the woman invited me to
an event at the Jack of Clubs.
'Why?'
'Because you're in the business.'
'What business is that?'
'The past business.'
Was it Lou? Was it someone she'd set up to make the call?
And then I recognised her as the blonde haired woman at the
club who toasted barflies.
'I hear you like the old times,' she continued.
I asked how she'd got my number.
'You're known.'
I tried to recall her face but realised I hadn't turned to look
at her at the bar. 'What's the event?'
'To keep the club going the way we like it – a fund-raising
evening of entertainment.'
'I didn't know the fifties personally.'
I realised I didn't even know who I was talking to. 'Who are you?'
'An illusionist.' She paused.
'What are you?' I insisted.

'I deal in illusion like you.'

I bet if I rang Kit I'd hear the reality of this fund-raising evening. There wasn't one.

*

Sadie Chill next on the line: 'I hear you want to know about Shanti Opal. She's the incarnation of a divinity. I told you before.'

'Where does the money come from?'

'From donations. She supports an ashram in India and other projects to bring enlightenment.'

'Have you met her?'

She paused. 'I have been in her presence.'

'Was there a woman, who could have been a model around her? Dark hair, hazel eyes, slightly slanted? Goes by the name of Lou or Eva Calvo Ludicci.'

She allowed a proper pause. 'Not when I was there.'

I didn't trust her either.

'We miss you, Isis. If you want a change you know where to come.'

I went back to Starlight and she held the snapshot to try, as she said, to get 'a connection'. 'Not what she seems.' She returned it as if she didn't want anymore to do with the subject. 'There's a lot of sadness. I wouldn't have expected that.' She rubbed her hands together as though cleansing them. 'Past life wasn't your thing, was it?'

'Past life? Isn't that what every reader says when they draw a blank?'

I walked back along the canal and on the other side of Gloucester Terrace I saw Ray standing with a woman. It took only a moment to remember where I'd seen her. The nice clothes, the light allure. Than I saw the cheroot. She turned in profile, laughing, and he laughed with her, quite relaxed, standing there together with a thousand past lives between them. Of course I had to wait for the oncoming van to pass before I could cross the road and when I had, of course they were gone. I rang his mobile and left a message. 'So the so-called chamber music enthusiast is still around. Could it be that she still wants a reading or are you giving her one?' I decided not to erase it.

I called the Jack of Clubs and the barman, said there was a fund-raising event in the pipeline. 'So we keep the lease.'

I asked about the woman who had called me and he said it could be one of the many supporters.

I called Ray, who was recording in West Hampstead, and asked if he had ever found out what happened to Eva Calvo Ludicci. 'Did you get back to the Ford Agency?'

'She dropped from sight.'

'Did you ask for a photograph?'

'Oh look, I thought you'd dropped all this.'

A lot of 'dropped' in this conversation. Was I next? He didn't mention the woman who smoked the cheroot.

*

I went to the club in the afternoon before dark because I was sure the fund-raising phone call had come from Lou. She hadn't appeared, it was true, but the invitation had her fingerprints, her contact was always provocative. I had to confront this Seraphim and her stratagem.

The bar was more crowded than it seemed, everything a little off-key. I said I wanted to speak to the person who was arranging the event. The barman was unsure. In the mirror I could see Kit's inner room, the door half open. It seemed to be empty. Why was I here? It was the word 'illusion'. 'I deal in illusion.' That made me sure it was her.

'Well, let's try the manager,' I suggested.

'Who shall I say?'

'Mrs Sheep.' I felt like adding 'whisky straight. Make it a double'.

The woman appeared too quickly. Even that was wrong. In no time at all she was at the doorway leading to the next flight of stairs and the upper room where the pagans held their moot.

She was not as tall as she should be and stood heavy with gravity, her feet solid on the ground. Her body didn't give away its shapes and lines under the thick jacket and long skirt. Even the clothes were weighted. The fair hair was pinned back, the eyes, not slanted at the corners, were blue. She wore glasses. The mouth was different, stretched in a smile that had nothing to do with pleasure. This was not Lou. I kept looking at her trying to find one aspect, one sign that this was the temptress from Rome. I stared as though she was a long lost child and I was being asked 'Is this her? Is this your daughter?' The forehead was too high. And then she stopped smiling and the clean, perfect teeth were covered up and her lips in repose were the give-away. You couldn't change those lips, not even collagen could do it. They were too perfect.

'I wanted to see you about the event.'

'Then you'll have to follow me.' The nice voice was measured. Where did she come from? If I asked she'd lie. This was the voice that I'd heard on my last visit offering drinks at the bar. She backed towards the stairs and I wasn't keen to go with her.

'What could I do exactly?'

'You could sing.' She said it nicely.

'I thought more about tarot reading.'

Her expression did not change. 'You could, but there are others who do that.'

A slight amusement now in the eyes and then their expression became distant, drawn far away to some other place of passion and longing as had happened on the train. Over that she had no control. She bent down and pretended to notice something out of place on the floor. She moved a chair, and so got away from my intruding gaze. Something in my face this time had alerted her. I knew and she knew it. She turned to the stairs and I saw she had much more hair than I'd expected.

'Come with me and we'll see what you can do.'

I held onto the bar as though to keep from obeying.

162

She hesitated and started up the stairs. My knuckles were white and I unclenched my fingers and in turn left the club, running.

I'd failed. I'd done it badly. I'd alerted her and would have to go back. And say what to this rather heavy creature with small but definite similarities to the sylph in the train? Yet she was older, even middle-aged. Too lost in thought I crossed Dean Street and nearly went under a car.

'You should look where you're going.'

He'd got that right.

*

I had to wait until the theatre emptied and then asked Ray to come with me. He was reluctant even angry, so I said I'd go on my own. I wished I'd asked Starlight.

'It's not a good idea getting into all that.'

'So what is all that suddenly? Obviously all that is something I haven't heard about.'

Of course it was in Lausanne, the something that had him so tired, wired and ever since different. And out of nowhere I knew what it was. 'Did you meet Lou?' I froze as I said it, the good old tarot reader's chill.

'It's not what you think.'

'I've got a very open mind. Tell me about it.'

He moved around irritated as though he had a right not to be questioned.

And then the unthinkable. 'You slept with her.'

'Oh no.' He couldn't shake his head enough and tried to approach me.

'Oh, so it was another sex partner. Do you know her name or didn't you have time to find out? Or something a little nearer home? The music enthusiast with the cheroot.'

'It's not what you think.'

I left the theatre laughing at the madness of it all. 'It's not what you think.' How do you know what I think? How many times on line hadn't I heard of guys cheating and found out saying to their partners these very words. He may have tried to catch me up but I crossed the courtyard alone and entered the club.

CHAPTER 21

'HOW MANY TIMES HAVE I tried to get you to meet the one who could have changed your life and how many times have you simply let me down?

And yet here you are visiting me without invitation. What a surprise.' And she leaned forward in the lamplight, not hiding the pale perfect face, the high forehead, the blue concentrated eyes and the give-away lips. How could this person be Lou, the punter on the line with the sheep taunts and the occasional rough voice who was also the exceptional woman on the train, her beauty not ever to be forgotten? As if aware of my question she flung off the body concealing thick jacket and that took years off her and made her perhaps a little more like Lou. She wasn't wearing glasses and the eyes were mesmerising, whatever colour. Yet this woman was older. Could Lou have aged so much since the journey to Reading a mere fifteen months ago?

'I'm surprised you dared to come,' she said.

We sat in Kit's inner room and the door was closed.

'But you're not Lou.' It had to be said.

'All you had to do was convince this life-exhausted man what way he should go and you'd have saved all this.' She paused. 'Possibly.'

I didn't like that. She had what they called in the business a big aura. Her presence filled the room. There was a power in this person that needed no demonstration.

'What you asked was not part of my job description.'

The power was coiled and still. She looked at me thoughtfully like a cat eyeing a mouse. Not the best look I'd ever seen.

'So what do you want?' she said.

'I'm tired of being used.'

'That's not an answer. I'm asking you what you want.'

Powerful? Worse.

Of course she could use disguise, but nothing was obvious. The touches of Lou, the lips, the farseeing expression and occasionally the presence had to have an explanation. Was this perhaps Lou's sister? At a pinch her mother?

'Why are you after me?'

'That presumably means the time before the "possibly". The days when you could have saved all this. Didn't you want money? You'd have certainly got it.'

I wanted to ask if she'd got it. If Mischa had finally chosen redemption, but I didn't feel safe with the question. There seemed to be something more disquieting in the air.

'What comes after "the possibly"?' I knew I wouldn't like it but I was on the main floor of the club, just a door between me and a crowd of fifties fans.

'Do you read thoughts?' I asked.

'I don't have to.' She moved papers around on the table and picked up a black and white photograph of a man lying by a door. On further inspection I saw he was also lying in a pool of blood. 'The police came and found the young singer a little out of it, the corpse and the gun.'

I could feel my thoughts as though dragged going towards the pale tulle skirt as it flicked across the blood. 'I never met him.'

I pushed the photograph back and expected she would speak. She sat in silence, her face shown to advantage by the light, the cheekbones high, eyes thoughtful.

'I just want to be left alone. My life is my own. No more

phone calls.' I nearly stood up ready to leave but realised I'd only dealt with the ordinary stuff. The other, the psychic attack was the main issue.

'I want to be free of all this – thought control – for instance the Seraphim's Stratagem.'

Her mouth twitched as though she found it amusing.

'You seem to want a lot, Isis. Years ago I wanted my career as a model. My contract with the Ford agency. I was doing well and had flown down from Milan for the party.'

'You told me all this on the train.' It didn't make her look any more like Lou. 'Didn't you?'

'I had a phenomenal career in front of me. Being there by the door with the corpse cost me that.'

So I asked why.

'Because it was known I was there. I could not be associated with that kind of party. The agency wouldn't like that. Ricco's associates didn't want me going around with a story to tell. So they simply finished me. Told the agency I was involved in a Mafia murder – Rinaldo from Jimmy's Bar believed I'd done it and promised he'd get me for it. So I had two problems: sudden career deprivation and a bar owner who wanted to kill me.'

It sounded all right but this woman wasn't the model Lou.

'I expect you're telling me all this for a good reason. Revenge. Blackmail.'

'No, simply to show you how most people want and they want it their way.'

'I can understand how disappointing your life must be and of course you still care and . . .'

'But I don't.'

I let that go. There were more urgent questions. 'So, who was the killer? I seem to have lost that role.'

'Ricco was a bad guy to attract. But he had his uses. He opened doors. It's a pity he couldn't open the one he blocked with his body that night, then everyone would have stayed as they were.'

I just hoped she wasn't going to say she was the killer. That would mean I'd never get out of there.

'So where is Lou?'

'Oh, she shows up from time to time.' She laughed and it wasn't unlike the sound I used to hear on the psychic line.

I stood up, ready to go.

'You don't look so good with all that make-up on.' She pushed across a box of tissues. I was still wearing my stage make-up, but my main problem was finding the door locked. This woman didn't seem as though she belonged to this story at all. This older, possibly wise person would never have been at that party.

'How did you get away from Rome?' Nearer to the door now; ready to shout if it was locked.

'You can go,' she said, simply.

Nothing was faster than my journey across the courtyard, along the alley and off into Dean Street.

Again Ray tried to ring me. He'd left a dozen messages. The woman with the cheroot was only a colleague. If I wanted proof I should do her cards. His last message suggested I get my own done.

I turned back to the Jack of Clubs and not without remembering a prayer pushed through the door. Each encounter with 'Lou' would be unsatisfactory and probably dangerous. I remembered Kit saying the Seraphim's Stratagem had to work its way out. I seemed to only stir things up.

She was sitting as I'd left her an hour earlier and didn't look up.

'How did you get to me?' I closed the door and stood against it.

'Your voice. Not immediately. You were Isis and somehow plausible. The worst clairvoyant in the world. Good on sheep. You needed money. Why else were you on line? Your voice allowed me to know you'd had a better life so something had gone wrong. Your voice was a one-off and would please my ex-protector. He'd go for that. And then I realised it was familiar.' She looked at me, waiting. What was she waiting for? 'Voices are Isis. Even from other times.' She waited to see if I had anything to say. 'I wondered where I'd heard it and then I knew.'

'You mean from my professional work.'

'Yes, that, and before.'

'Oh, you mean Rome. What else is there?'

'Before even that.'

I didn't understand her. I chanced a question, 'How did you get away from Rome?'

'The banker Mischa took care of it. I dropped out. And then recently his ailing spirituality needed a shot from the next realms so I used you.'

I didn't like the way she was answering so openly. When did we get to the closed?

'You became evasive, so I simply tracked you down and there we are.'

'But if I'd have gone to him with a pack of cards and your messages that would not have been it.'

'No, not after 'the possibly'.'

She sat quite still, looking at me, assessing me, as though deciding what to do.

'The murder . . . the murder,' and I tried to get her mind elsewhere, 'You tried to stick that on me. You've put me in danger.'

'Oh, that doesn't matter anymore.' She sounded quite light-hearted and then moved a hand through her hair and I was terrified, terrified it would loosen the blonde hair, reveal it as a wig and underneath Lou's dark chignon.

'You said you wanted your career. What do you mean you don't want it now? And the murder doesn't matter. What are you saying?'

And the hand without rings moved faster across the hair. Once again I left the place running.

✳

Kit had only seen the woman who was organising the fifties event in the past days. It was rumoured she had been an investor for some years and owned the leasehold. Kit did not find her powerful or beautiful and in fact she seemed to blend into any background.

'Exactly.' I needed to know who she was and the probable outcome, and asked what would be my best defence. Kit handed me a pack of cards and Starlight said there might be news of Shanti Opal. One of the readers on line had seen her in London.

'Oh yes,' said Elmore. 'I saw a woman most fleetingly in the vegetarian restaurant, and the owner said she looked like Shanti Opal. Someone else said oh, she's still around. Somewhere hidden in the Far East.' He laughed. 'As I said you don't need to go so far. You can hide even in the spotlight.'

I asked which vegetarian restaurant and he said the one in Primrose Hill.

'Did Lou get to her?' I asked.

Kit looked at me, baffled, and even allowed a pause while shuffling the cards to register my stupidity. 'The Seraphim's Stratagem' and she laid out seven cards. 'You must remember the Seraphim is an angel, dark or otherwise. You have known her once.' She closed the cards and I waited for another spread. No spread. She folded her hands and leaned forward ready to give stern news, probably coloured by aspects from Saturn.

'You're in it and you have to see it through.'

'But what is this Stratagem? Am I in danger?' I turned to Elmore. 'Please.'

He laid out from memory the original cards I'd found outside my flat, then placed them in a hexagram. Pointing to the middle card he said, 'That's the player. The initiate. But she's no longer there.' He indicated the Queen of Diamonds on a lower line further off. 'So she is moving on and away and when she gets to here . . .' he pointed to the bottom edge, 'it's over.'

'But what is it? The Seraphim's Strategem?'

'The gateway. The portal. To the uninitiated it can look like a cage in a series of reflections.' He stabbed a finger at the central card. 'This connects here to there. This reality to other states of being. It's a passageway. Through this the initiate moves to and fro sending ritual signs.'

'Such as?'

'Love, threats, or symbols such as the ladder, the sword, the key, a bird waiting. She can activate the past. This life, another life. It's an abundant passage and a high initiate can go through the gateway to other realms.'

I had never heard of the gateway or portal.

'It can be an unmoving location on the planet where the atmosphere or skin of the earth is thin and there are sufficient energy pulses and ley lines. There you can have a gateway from this world to other constellations. It is only visible if the initiate resonates with the energy.'

'Oh, a wormhole.'

'Not exactly. But she, the Seraphim, can sometimes produce this space and time transformation in any locale by her attunement.'

'So I'd get my past back?'

'Or your future.'

✳

Ray's coming in made me jump to my feet which was a good barometer of how fraught my nerves were these days.

'Go on like that and you don't need to diet.'

'She's not Lou.'

He threw down his bag. The violin case got better treatment.

'I wonder what became of her,' I said.

'She became a guru.'

Why hadn't I seen it, expected it? Kit had seen it. Was that why she looked at me earlier with such disbelief?

'She was good business and made a bundle for them. The banker and his associates. They rescued her in Rome and cleaned away her past, got rid of the agency data, the photographs. Left a fake PR. Couldn't do much with the glossy mags. Already out. She'd only been going six months. They had to hide her somewhere. What better than the guru role? Sometimes she didn't even have to speak. She did it for years, but times change and as they say, the tidal wave of the guru cult is over. They were going to fade her out. She'd served her purpose.'

'Did she tell you this?'

'She became too uncontrollable for them. Of course she's fake but she started to believe her own stuff. She'd made them money so she wanted hers and plenty of it. She was too dangerous and the banker backed out. He'd been her lover and got scared of her. She certainly worked on him because he didn't know or not whether there was an after-world and what it would do to him. She'd started using hypnotic practices so he experienced things he could not explain. Then she turns him over to you. She suggests he try a psychic line. It's neutral and she and her associate, known as the brother, set up the connection. But he wouldn't go for it and then she recognised your voice. So she had you. It's all over.'

*

He took me by surprise with that. I wished it was. I got the snapshot from my bag. Was it Lou? No jagged teeth. Long fair hair in ringlets. No slant to hazel eyes.

'Lou,' he spoke quickly, 'has hair dyed black and styled lower over the forehead. The hazel eyes, courtesy of contact lenses, are lifted very slightly at the corners by pins at the side of her face hidden in hair. Lifts increase height and throw weight forward. Bridge with four jagged teeth and one gold one take all the attention and are attached over real teeth like a denture. This bridge makes her upper jaw more prominent and changes face shape. Cannot change lips it seems. Make-up does the rest. Shanti Opal. Bridge attachment off. Mouth not so forward because no teeth protruding. Natural high forehead, hair rinsed blonde often in ringlets with extensions. Eyes naturally cornflower blue. The slight slanting gone with removal of pins. Remove lifts and walk is normal, she becomes shorter. Make-up especially shading does the rest. The padded clothes make her older. She learned the guru manner of speech and behaviour along the way. She says she was born on the right side of the tracks but couldn't wait to get to the wrong side. They tried to drop her. She wasn't having dropped.

'Good? Bad?'

'Deadly.'

I slumped silently at the table. I kept thinking what bad luck. Why did I ever become a telephone psychic? 'Is this the whole story?' I didn't think so.

He pushed across a photo of Lou as a model, sultry, inviting, wonderful body, but the lips would always get the attention.

'She shot Ricco?'

'That's why they covered her all these years. Ricco made a wrong play for a girl and Lou got upset. Something like that. He died with Lou squashed under him. At first she couldn't get out. Rinaldo at Jimmy's Bar knew the truth. Others who wanted him dead called it Mafia.'

'So what did she do? Give you a spiritual evolvement one to one.'

He ignored the chance for another row and spoke gently. 'The banker had been telling me how dangerous she is and I did not want you in it. I realise she's not a master of disguise but a chameleon. She creates these different appearances to survive and if she can changes her whole personality.'

I thought of lesser players, Vinnie and Mrs Longbridge, but there was always one sound or speech rhythm that gave it away.

'Where did she pick you up?'

'Near his place. I didn't recognise her from your description of the girl on the train. Nor did the banker. Not at first. She told me something that frightened me, something that in ordinary circumstances I could not believe. Please believe me.'

'What was it?'

'Something about the dream you used to have.'

And I looked at his eyes, into them. It wasn't over.

∗

I saw the cage of yellow light and in the middle a fair girl on a swing calling to me. She seemed so young. And then the sound of the body falling hard on the road, and the eyeball rolling towards the kerb. The scream always came first. I heard Lou say something that defined this dream and I thought I must never forget those words.

CHAPTER 22

I DIDN'T HEAR FROM her and I couldn't believe it. Twice I'd stopped by the club and left a message. I wanted it cleared, once and for all. I didn't like the 'possibly' and the before and after conditions. Or 'your voice – I wondered where I'd heard it and then I knew.' The professional world? Rome? It hadn't sounded like it. Earlier. What was earlier?

Some days later I thought I saw her on Primrose Hill. She was walking down as I was going up. She came over the top of the hill towards me with the detachment of a sleepwalker and a smile, a small private one as though she hadn't seen me. And for a moment there was no one else around. It was cold and damp, a bad November day. And she wore old-fashioned, sinister clothes, galoshes, a headscarf. I did wonder if she was a ghost. I turned and she was still moving as though in a trance towards the main path before the flat ground began.

Back at the club, I sat drinking tonic and lemon and felt safe because Kit was in her room giving readings. As always the place was lively. The barman said he hadn't seen the fundraiser for a few days. He wouldn't say anymore about her, not even her name. Two electricians fixing the wiring took his attention. Lights flashed on, then off, as the fault spread.

I felt the chill, the old psychic telephone line shiver and looked behind me. She was in the corridor by the stairs indicating I join her. Thinking it safe, I went towards her but not close.

'You give yourself away,' I said. 'In your last Albert Hall gig an American touch, just one. They say yours is a voice you'd want to hear as you lay dying. Where are you from? Chicago?'

She was watching me not without a certain tenderness.

'How do you do it? The guru thing?'

'Like you. Just get in to them, they listen and then you've got them.'

'Yet you know something. Like myths and Mother Shipton, Primrose Hill. How do you know that?'

'Ley lines, earth energies – I know about these things. I had enough years learning it.'

It was different today. Extraordinary but true, we were like lovers re-meeting.

'You were Ricco's mistress,' I said.

'Oh, don't go on about him. He was such a lustful pest, hands always over somebody's legs, in their clothes.'

'You were jealous and that's why you killed him.'

'Not a chance.' A little rough, almost Lou now. 'He was pestering a girl.'

'And you were jealous.'

'I loved her.'

I thought I hadn't heard correctly and got her to repeat it.

'But the girl was all out of it and couldn't handle herself.'

Not me. Definitely not me. 'But you knew her.'

'I had once.'

She changed her tone, her energy. 'So if you want to be with me you have to follow me.' And around her the yellow bars became visible, strengthened and filled with light, and how I wished they wouldn't. And she was like the girl on the swing and I like something in a dream from which I could not awake.

'You're just a fake. You trick. It's all an illusion.' I shouted so loud even Kit must have heard. I shouted to free myself.

'We both deal in illusion. We purvey a mysterious other and it's a trick. What else?'

'You're evil. You killed the Italian. You took Ray. I'll get you for that.'

'Come and get me.' She laughed.

Furious I rushed into the cage of light and it seemed to encase me, then grip me painfully. It turned into a network of gold corridors twisting and turning endlessly. I tried to catch her but she was always one corridor ahead, laughing, taunting. I could hear the sound of her shoes.

'What comes after 'the possible',' I cried.

'You're in it.'

'What is this?' I was breathless.

'The portal.'

'What?' Should I stop? Go back?

'The gateway between here and there.' And then I couldn't hear the shoes.

'I don't want you,' I shouted. 'You will never get me.'

Around the next corner she was waiting still and deadly. A barred shadow fell across her face. And for a moment I felt pity for her.

'Were you always like this? It's not . . .'

'It is. Too late.' She didn't mess with the truth when it was hers.

I held out my hand and she shrivelled backwards, her eyes changing as though she was frightened of the changes happening inside her. 'You always were a goody-two-shoes.' The eyes full of corridors closing, opening like the shutters of an old camera.

All I had to do was remove my life from hers. As I watched she seemed to shrink, to crumble, become dust. Like something unearthly becoming extinct. She could barely speak. 'I just wanted you one more time.'

Terrified I ran along the corridors sharp-edged with glittering artificial light. And the corridor became a chamber with an ordinary door opening onto another light, harsh daytime glare. Into the street and I knew it was Rome. And then I recognised it was the fifties.

'But I love you.' She was beside me and dressed in 1950s clothes, beautiful, innocent.

'It's wrong.' I couldn't bear it and ran away across the street and she came after me and grabbed my arm.

'I won't let you go,' she promised. I could hear the car. 'Ever.'

The metal ploughed into us and we lay broken, her leg, part of mine, she breathed for both of us, her eye in my mouth, my absent cheek filling with her blood, truly together. We could never be so close in life as this, which dying allowed.

'I'll look for you in every life.'

These were the last words of the dream.

✳

I came to in the courtyard and Ray was rubbing my numb hands. I could hear a lively noise from the club.

'I've told you, don't go near that place.'

I was half sitting on the bench terrified of what was left of me. Was I whole? Injured?

'They had an electricity blowout. A wiring problem. They thought you got an electric shock.' He waited for me to remember it.

'You can speak,' he said.

But I could not.

✳

I did just manage the show the following night and when I wouldn't go near the pub Ray tried again to speak to me. It took another night before I could let myself listen to what he'd experienced on the visit to Lausanne. It seemed she had accosted him near the banker's home and talked of a life in the past I had shared with her and that this one would end badly if not resolved. He must keep out of it. He kept saying how he didn't believe things like this and it wasn't a part of reality as he understood it. But in spite of all he believed he sensed truth in what she said. She must have induced some kind of trance state there and then, because he saw something happen in the street where they were standing and there was something wrong with it. There was an accident but immediately afterwards there was no sign of what he'd just seen. 'So don't go near her,' she'd warned him. Shaken up, he'd asked how she'd known me before. 'Oh a past life of passion. Forbidden naturally,' she replied, insolently. I asked for details of the accident but he wasn't keen on details. He kept saying the clothes weren't right. 'Yes, they wore fifties clothes,' I said.

Some hours later, he said nothing had been right. It was like a moment stuck in time. The bodies in bits, flung about all mixed up as though in a modern painting. 'Like that dream you had?'

Elmore watched Kit lay out the old spread. 'The Seraphim's Stratagem only lasts a certain time. It's faded. She's gone,' he said.

'Gone where?'

'To spirit.'

'How do you know?'

'The cage is empty.'

*

Months later I'd finished the new show and was leaving the theatre. I signed an autograph and went towards the car. A woman approached without my even noticing her. 'Could you read my cards?'

I almost stopped. 'I don't do that anymore.'

I turned and tried to see her face. She was wrapped in some kind of scarf.

'What a shame. I heard you were good on sheep.'

Lightning Source UK Ltd.
Milton Keynes UK
UKOW04f1444120615

253407UK00002B/21/P